WHY WE WENT EXTINCT

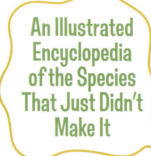

An Illustrated Encyclopedia of the Species That Just Didn't Make It

By TADAAKI IMAIZUMI and TAKASHI MARUYAMA
Illustrated by MASANORI SATO, YOKO UETAKE, KENTA KAIDO, and NASUMISOITAME
Translated by ANGUS TURVILL

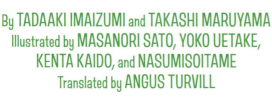

CONTENTS

Foreword viii

We All Went Extinct x

Animals Are Powerless Against the Earth xii

Survival Is Tough xiv

Is Extinction Sad? xvi

But, Of Course, We Don't Want to Go Extinct! ... xviii

How to Enjoy This Book xx

PART 1: Caught Unprepared

- **STELLER'S SEA COW** (Too kind) 2
- **DODO** (Too slow) 4
- **GIGANTOPITHECUS** (Lost out to pandas) 6
- **ICHTHYOSAUR** (Not enough squid) 8
- **BONIN GROSBEAK** (The goats ate everything) 10
- **SPINOSAURUS** (Couldn't get out of the river) 12
- **ARTHROPLEURA** (A slow eater) 14
- **LYALL'S WREN** (Wiped out by a cat) 16
- **SOUTHERN GASTRIC-BROODING FROG** (Mold) 18
- **GIANT MOA** (Swallowing stones) 20
- **DICKINSONIA** (Too soft) 22
- **PIG-FOOTED BANDICOOT** (Attacked by foxes) 24
- **JAPANESE WOLF** (Infected by dogs) 26
- **TASMANIAN WOLF** (Took the blame for dogs' crimes) .. 28
- **DIATRYMA** (Didn't look after its eggs) 30
- **MEGATHERIUM** (No enemies) 32

PART 2: Just Too Extra

- **PLATYBELODON** (Chin too heavy) 36
- **HELICOPRION** (Teeth didn't come out) 38
- **PASSENGER PIGEON** (Too many) 40
- **CAMEROCERAS** (Too straight) 42
- **NIPPONITES** (In a tangle) 44
- **BLUEBUCK** (Too beautiful) 46
- **OPABINIA** (Too much ornament) 48
- **TARPAN** (A love affair with a horse) 50
- **IRISH ELK** (Antlers took all nutrients) 52
- **BOW-BEAKED HAWAIIAN HONEYCREEPER** (Beak too specialized) 54
- **MEGANEURA** (Couldn't breathe) 56
- **THYLACOSMILUS** (Too stupid) 58
- **TITANOBOA** (Couldn't cope with heat or cold) ... 60
- **SCHOMBURGK'S DEER** (Antlers too splendid) .. 62
- **DIMETRODON** (Sail fin got in the way) 64
- **MAMENCHISAURUS** (Neck too long) 66

PART 3: So Awkward

- **ARCHAEOPTERYX** (Couldn't fly properly)...... 70
- **SABER-TOOTHED TIGER** (Too muscular)....... 72
- **MEGALODON** (Whales hit back).............. 74
- **ANOMALOCARIS** (Weak teeth)................ 76
- **PARACERATHERIUM** (Ate too much).......... 78
- **DUNKLEOSTEUS** (Not enough oxygen)........ 80
- **ARGENTAVIS** (Wind stopped blowing)........ 82
- **PAKICETUS** (Neither one thing nor the other)... 84
- **GIANT PENGUIN** (Whales came to the Antarctic). 86
- **SIVATHERIUM** (Eating grass)................ 88
- **MASTODONSAURUS** (Dried out).............. 90
- **ICHTHYOSTEGA**
  (Came up onto land for no real reason)...... 92

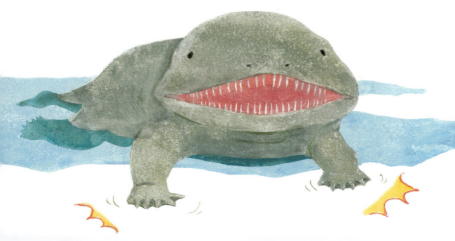

PART 4: Out of Luck

- **TYRANNOSAURUS** (Meteorite strike) 96
- **GREAT AUK** (Island sank) 98
- **BAIJI (CHINESE RIVER DOLPHIN)** (Dirty river) .. 100
- **POLYNESIAN TREE SNAIL** (Snail warfare) 102
- **SEA SCORPION (EURYPTERID)** (Magma misery) . 104
- **ANDREWSARCHUS** (Everest got higher) 106
- **TOYOTAMAPHIMEIA** (Couldn't escape cold) ... 108
- **CONODONT** (Water got hot) 110
- **WOOLLY MAMMOTH** (Snowfall) 112
- **CUBAN RED MACAW** (Blown away by a hurricane) .. 114
- **LAUGHING OWL** (Laughed too much) 116
- **TRILOBITE** (Eaten by fish) 118
- **ARSINOITHERIUM** (Stranded in the desert) ... 120
- **GUAM FLYING FOX** (Eaten out of curiosity) ... 122
- **STEGOSAURUS** (Blooming flowers) 124

PART 5: Made It Out Alive

- DUCK-BILLED PLATYPUS (Got into water) 128
- PTARMIGAN (Went to the mountains) 130
- PYGMY HIPPOPOTAMUS (Stayed in the woods) .. 132
- TUATARA (Low profile—long life) 134
- NAUTILUS (Couldn't be bothered) 136
- TREE LOBSTER (Crossed the sea on driftwood) . 138
- COELACANTH (Strayed into the deep) 140
- OPOSSUM (Slow to evolve) 142
- BLACK KOKANEE
  (Was somewhere else all along) 144
- LUNGFISH (Stayed in a burrow) 146

Afterword 148

Index 150

Foreword

Extinction is when a species disappears forever from Earth.

That definition makes it sound terrible, but if you look at the history of living things, you realize extinction isn't all bad. Of course, animals haven't wanted to become extinct. But after major extinctions, other creatures have a chance to undergo great evolutionary change.

For example, the extinction of the dinosaurs led to astonishing evolution among birds and mammals. From the creatures that survived major extinction events came the next generations of animals.

It was a similar story for the human species. When forests shrank, giving way to grassland, many apes became extinct. Humankind developed from those that survived.

Extinction is a mechanism of nature. But many species' extinctions have also been brought about by humans. And unlike the ones that happen as a result of nature, human-caused extinctions don't lead to new evolution.

This book tells the stories of many different animals that have gone extinct. I hope that it will encourage readers to think about all the different reasons why extinction happens.

—TADAAKI IMAIZUMI

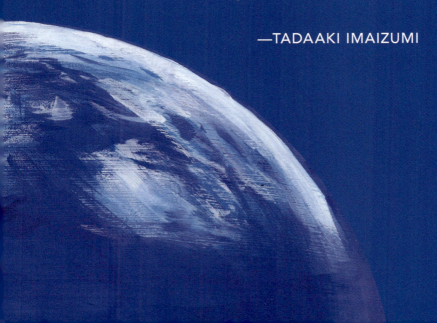

We All Went Extinct

Life first developed on Earth about four billion years ago.

It seems that a single cell—the smallest unit of life, invisible to the naked eye—developed by chance in the sea. This was the start of all life on Earth.

But if there's a start, there will always be an end.

The end of life is death. And the end of a species is extinction.

Extinction means the disappearance from the world of every creature of a species.

Many strong species and many clever species no longer exist.

So why did they die out?

Animals Are Powerless Against the Earth

There are two types of reasons for extinction:
1. The earth
2. Other creatures

The overwhelming majority of extinctions happen because of the earth. Whenever the environment has changed greatly, most creatures living there at the time have died out. We call these periods of change "extinction events." And each one has resulted in major changes to the profile of species on Earth. Those that survive are just the lucky ones that happen to have escaped harm.

When you're up against the earth, strength or weakness make no difference at all.

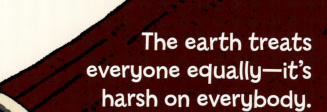

The earth treats everyone equally—it's harsh on everybody.

Causes of extinction ranked

1ST (BY A LOT)
EXTREME CHANGES TO THE ENVIRONMENT

Volcanic eruptions, falling meteorites, changes in temperature that bring severe heat or cold, loss of oxygen . . . Events like these alter the environment so much that, no matter what, animals have no chance of surviving.

2ND
A RIVAL COMES ON THE SCENE

A species can go extinct when a rival appears—one that is nimbler, cleverer, or more energy-efficient—and edges the older species out of its food and habitat. (Sometimes the rival has developed from the original species' own descendants!)

3RD
HUMANS

No creature has destroyed as many fellow species as humans have. They have caused extinction by overhunting or by changing the environment. Still, the proportion of extinctions caused by humans is low compared to the other two causes.

Survival Is Tough

It wouldn't be possible to survive these kinds of extreme changes to the environment, would it? In fact, 99.9 percent of all the species that have lived on Earth are now extinct.

The whole earth freezes.

HOW EXTINCTION EVENTS HAPPENED!

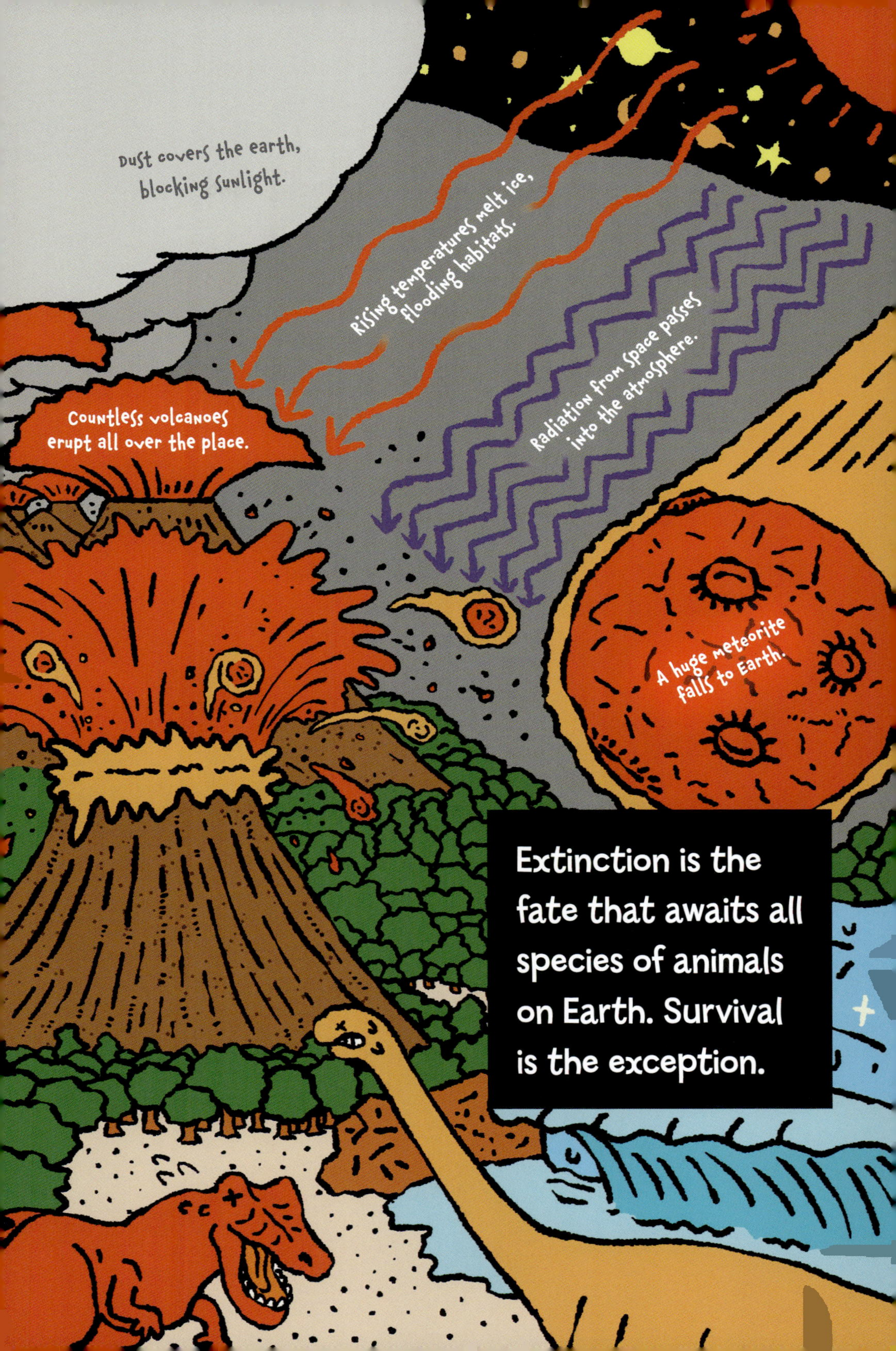
Dust covers the earth, blocking sunlight.
Rising temperatures melt ice, flooding habitats.
Radiation from space passes into the atmosphere.
Countless volcanoes erupt all over the place.
A huge meteorite falls to Earth.

Extinction is the fate that awaits all species of animals on Earth. Survival is the exception.

Is Extinction Sad?

Not necessarily. Extinction isn't always a bad thing.

There's a limit to how many animals can live on Earth. There are limits to resources of air, water, and soil, so a population's numbers can't keep increasing forever.

It's like all animal species are playing musical chairs. If there's no empty chair in a habitat—if established species are already using all the resources available—then there's no chance for a new species to establish itself and thrive.

Extinction and evolution are closely connected.

But, Of Course, We Don't Want to Go Extinct!

Extinction comes to all types of creatures. All are treated equally.

It may even be lurking in the shadows, reaching out for you and the rest of humanity as you read this book.

But we humans have weapons that we can use against extinction: study and thought. If we learn how different animals became extinct, we may be able to think of ways to keep surviving on Earth in the future.

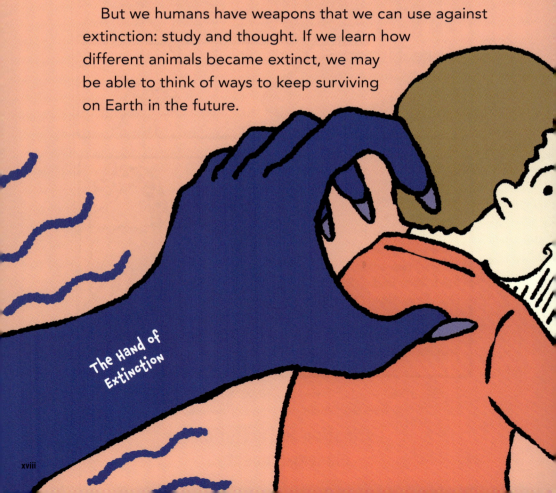

The Hand of Extinction

Let's hear from the extinct animals themselves about what happened to them!

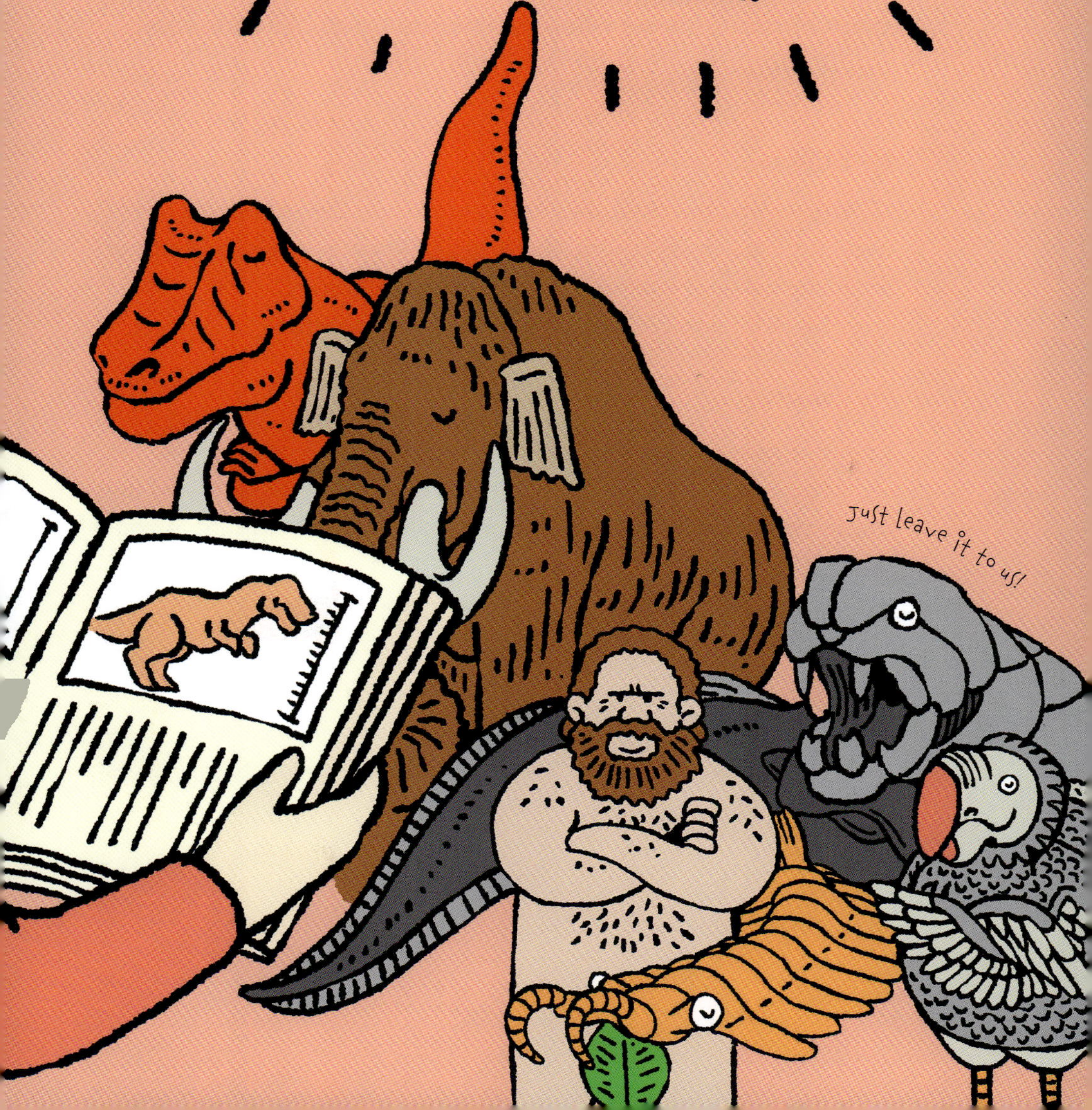
Just leave it to us!

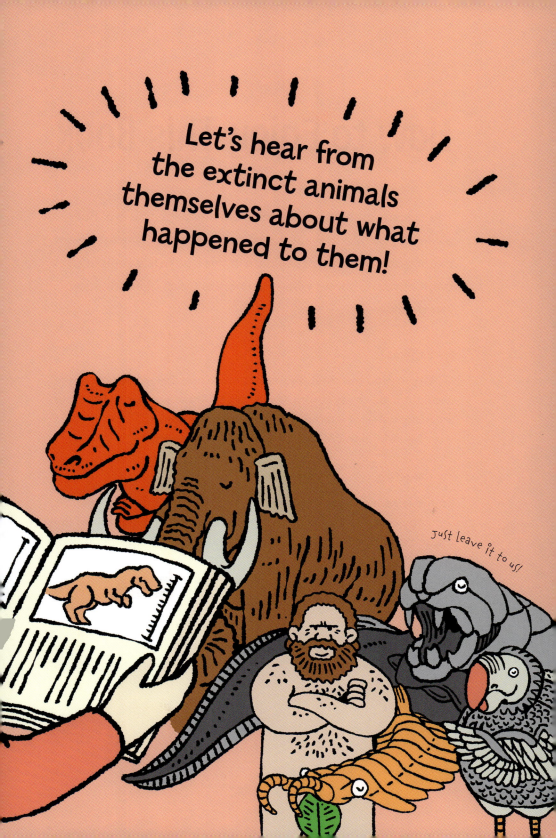

How to Enjoy This Book

You can start reading this book from any page you like. But always try to take in what the animals say about why they went extinct. You'll find plenty of data in this book. The sample page opposite shows where to find the types of information listed below.

1. Basic data

This gives you the creature's appearance and size, what part of the world it lived in, et cetera. You'll get to know some details about each animal—for example, what it ate or its home habitat. It could also be helpful to compare one animal with another.

2. Comments

In these sections, you'll find more information about the animal's ecology and why it went extinct. If you read the comments and the basic data together, it may help you to build up a picture in your mind of each animal.

3. Period of existence

This shows you when the creature appeared and when it went extinct so at a glance you'll have a rough idea of when it was alive and how long it survived. Some lasted a very long time; others disappeared very quickly.

Go on! Have a browse!

We are living in the Cenozoic era. The Cenozoic era is divided into three periods, then divided further into seven epochs. It becomes rather complicated, so we haven't included the epochs in the full chart you'll see throughout the book, but it is good to know them in order to obtain more detailed information about extinction.

xxi

We were grand

        It simply ain't fair

Whoa-oh,

        we weren't prepared . . .

Just not vigilant enough...

PART 1

Caught Unprepared

All creatures have their heyday.
But it doesn't last forever.
One careless moment, and extinction
may be right there in front of you.

I was living in the sea up near the North Pole. There were two thousand of us there. What a happy time it was! Eating kelp all day every day. No fights, no arguments. Just munching kelp—it was like munching happiness itself. It may sound a bit dull, I suppose, but it was so peaceful!

One day, a bunch of boats appeared. Some humans traveling through our territory had happened to catch one of us in a net. They'd eaten our poor friend, and rumor had spread that the meat was very tasty. Now all these other humans had come to get some. They wanted our skins as well.

We tried to get away, of course, but we couldn't swim very fast. Not surprising, really, for kelp eaters. And we couldn't bear to leave anybody behind if they got injured. If one of us was attacked, we gathered around them to try to help. And that just made it easy for the humans to catch a lot of us at the same time.

Regrets?
If we'd been faster swimmers, we might have been able to escape our new predators.

YEAR OF EXTINCTION	1768
SIZE	26 feet (7.9 meters) body length
AREA	North Pacific (Bering Sea)
FOOD	Seaweed
TYPE	Mammal

A large maritime mammal with substantial reserves of fat, well adapted to life in cold seas. Dugongs and manatees alive today eat sea plants with their molars. Steller's sea cows had no teeth and used their gums instead. They were easy for humans to catch because they gathered together to help each other if one of them was attacked. They became extinct just twenty-seven years after they were discovered by explorers.

PRECAMBRIAN | PALEOZOIC ERA (CAMBRIAN PERIOD, ORDOVICIAN PERIOD, SILURIAN PERIOD, DEVONIAN PERIOD, CARBONIFEROUS PERIOD, PERMIAN PERIOD) | MESOZOIC ERA (TRIASSIC PERIOD, JURASSIC PERIOD, CRETACEOUS PERIOD) | CENOZOIC ERA (PALEOGENE PERIOD, NEOGENE PERIOD, QUATERNARY PERIOD)

STELLER'S SEA COW

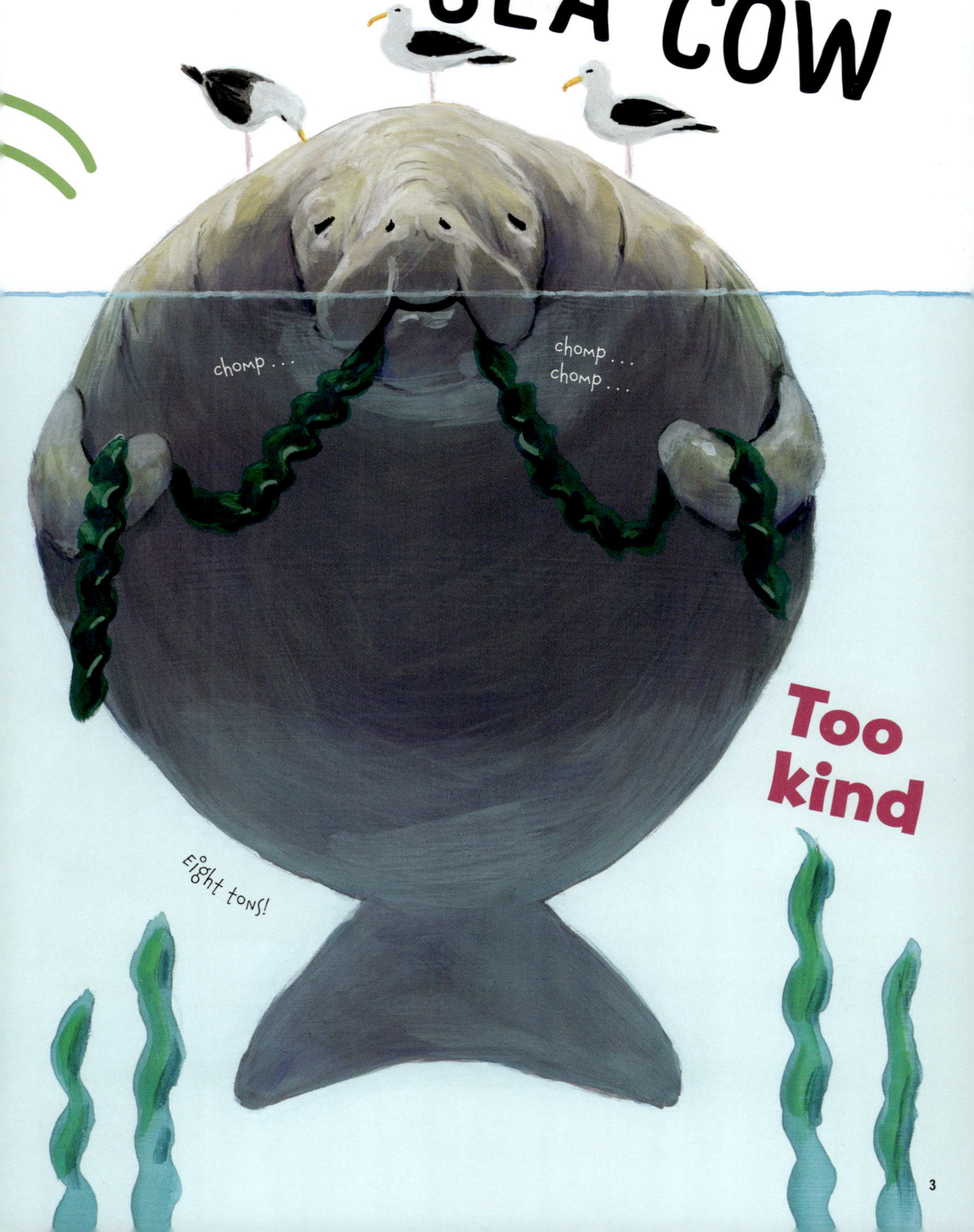
chomp . . .
chomp . . .
chomp . . .
Eight tons!

Too kind

Well, yeah, we went extinct. What? Too easygoing? Mm . . . You're not the first to say that.

We lived on a small island off Africa, and just over four hundred years ago, a lot of ships started arriving from different countries. And soon, we found humans coming up close to where we lived. *Well*, we thought, *what's going on?* And we wandered over toward them. But before we knew it, they were eating us up! What a shock!

Regrets?
We should have been more careful—by hiding our eggs in holes, for one thing.

YEAR OF EXTINCTION	1681
SIZE	3 feet (0.9 meter) total length
AREA	Mauritius
FOOD	Fruit
TYPE	Bird

They didn't look like it, but dodos were a close relative of pigeons. Their ancestors probably flew to Mauritius from mainland Africa and then, without any natural predators on the island, they grew bigger and lost the ability to fly. The island of Mauritius was formed by a volcanic eruption out in the ocean, and it's a long way from anywhere else. The only mammals that had managed to get there were bats. Dodos had lived in a safe environment for so long that when humans suddenly appeared, they showed no caution at all.

Tortoises are quicker.

PRECAMBRIAN	PALEOZOIC ERA						MESOZOIC ERA			CENOZOIC ERA		
	CAMBRIAN PERIOD	ORDOVICIAN PERIOD	SILURIAN PERIOD	DEVONIAN PERIOD	CARBONIFEROUS PERIOD	PERMIAN PERIOD	TRIASSIC PERIOD	JURASSIC PERIOD	CRETACEOUS PERIOD	PALEOGENE PERIOD	NEOGENE PERIOD	QUATERNARY PERIOD

We'd never had an enemy before. We couldn't fly, and we couldn't run, so they could pick us up with their bare hands, just like that. They sometimes took two hundred of us in a day! And it wasn't just the humans—they brought to the island dogs and rats, which ate our eggs. We always laid them on the ground. We didn't really think about protecting them. . . .

DODO

Too slow

Laid its eggs anywhere

Oh dear! I feel like I haven't eaten a thing! I'm big, I know, and I look like a bruiser, but I'm *strictly* vegetarian. At first, we lived in forests, in what you now call China. Oh, we used to stuff ourselves with fruit!

But then the forest shrank—at least the part that was suitable for us to live in—and we couldn't get enough fruit anymore! Then we noticed bamboo. . . . I wasn't sure about it *at all*! I could feel the other animals' eyes on me, like, *Ooh! She's going to eat bamboo!* They were snickering, I'm sure. Bamboo's not nutritious, you see, so none of them ever ate it.

But I went ahead. I swallowed my pride and ate.

It was then that they arrived—the pandas! They look cute, but they eat *so* much bamboo! There just wasn't enough to go around. And in the end, we went extinct.

Regrets?
We should have moved away and found something else to eat besides bamboo.

TIME OF EXTINCTION	Quaternary period (late Pleistocene epoch)
SIZE	10 feet (3 meters) tall
AREA	Asia
FOOD	Plants
TYPE	Mammal

As the largest-ever primate, the gigantopithecus was a relative of modern humans. However, the only fossils that have been found are of its huge lower jaw and teeth, so we don't know for sure how big it was or what it looked like. In the Quaternary period, the climate became colder and the amount of forest shrank, so the gigantopithecus didn't have enough food. They began to eat broadleaf bamboo, a fast-growing plant that tolerates cold. But it's thought that the bamboo didn't provide them with enough nutrition to save them from extinction.

PRECAMBRIAN	PALEOZOIC ERA						MESOZOIC ERA			CENOZOIC ERA		
	CAMBRIAN PERIOD	ORDOVICIAN PERIOD	SILURIAN PERIOD	DEVONIAN PERIOD	CARBONIFEROUS PERIOD	PERMIAN PERIOD	TRIASSIC PERIOD	JURASSIC PERIOD	CRETACEOUS PERIOD	PALEOGENE PERIOD	NEOGENE PERIOD	QUATERNARY PERIOD

GIGANTOPITHECUS

Lost out to pandas

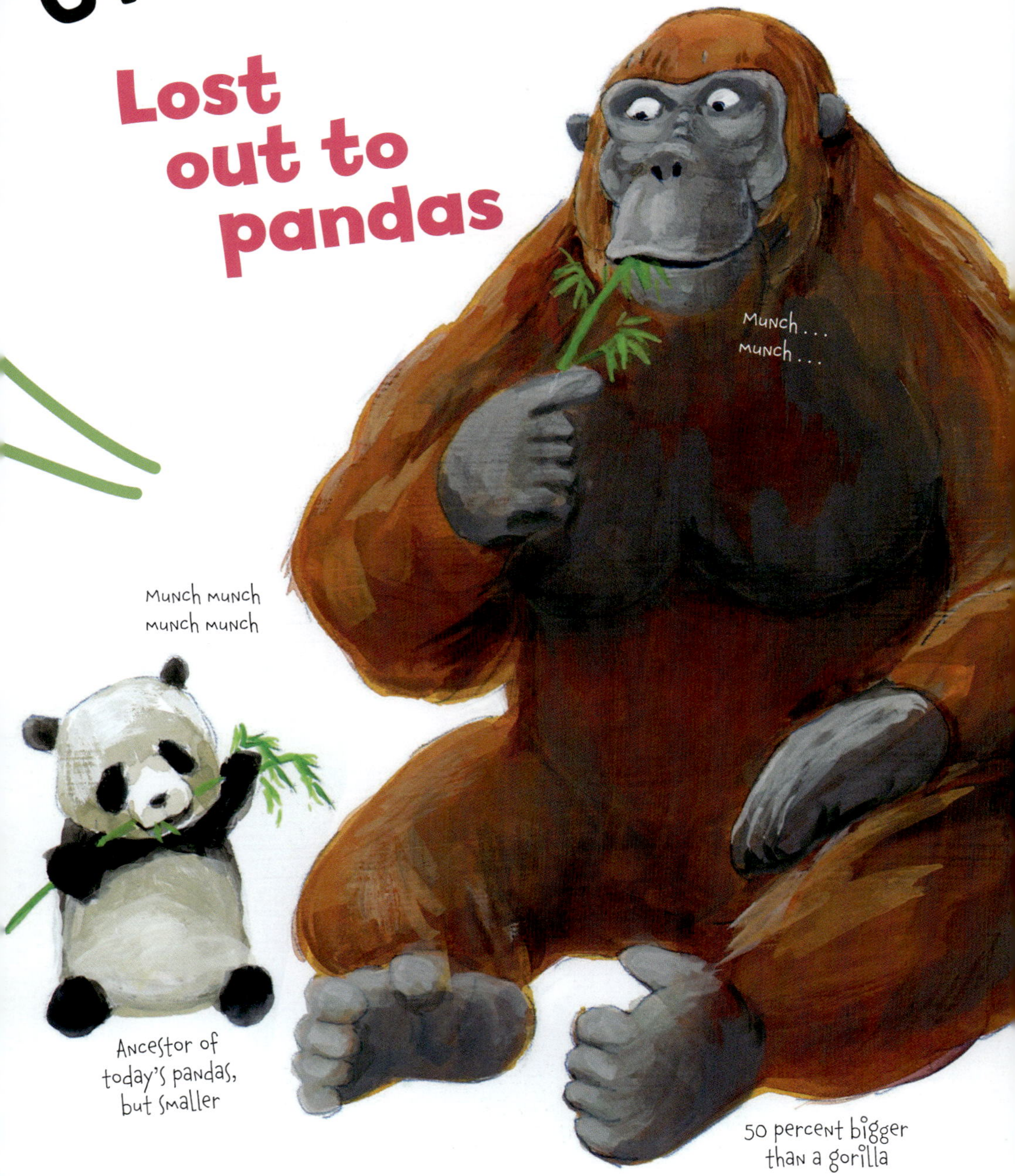

Munch . . .
munch . . .
Munch munch
munch munch
Ancestor of today's pandas, but smaller
50 percent bigger than a gorilla

Curdling cuttlefish! Not a squid to be seen! After that seabed volcano erupted, they all died. Squid was all we ate. We don't know how to catch anything else. . . . What could we do?

What do you mean, *Why not eat fish?* Hunt them with *ultrasound*? You're thinking of dolphins, my friend. I'm not a flipping dolphin. I'm an ichthyosaur! I use my eyes. I keep watch. We took charge of the ocean 250 million

Regrets?
We shouldN't have been such fussy eaters!

A lovely squid

Delicious!

The ichthyosaur, a reptile, flourished in the ocean during the Mesozoic era, when dinosaurs dominated on land. One theory links the ichthyosaur's extinction to the eruptions of seabed volcanoes, which severely impacted sea-water oxygen levels. The loss of oxygen is thought to have decimated the population of Belemnitidae, a squid-like cephalopod that was the ichthyosaur's main food. As a result, the ichthyosaurs died of starvation.

(By the way, dolphins evolved in a very similar environment to that of the ichthyosaurs and so look similar, but they are completely different types of animal.)

TIME OF EXTINCTION	Mid-Cretaceous period
SIZE	1 to 70 feet (0.3 to 21 meters) total length
AREA	Oceans all over the world
FOOD	Belemnitidae
TYPE	Reptile

PRECAMBRIAN	PALEOZOIC ERA	MESOZOIC ERA	CENOZOIC ERA
	CAMBRIAN PERIOD / ORDOVICIAN PERIOD / SILURIAN PERIOD / DEVONIAN PERIOD / CARBONIFEROUS PERIOD / PERMIAN PERIOD	TRIASSIC PERIOD / JURASSIC PERIOD / CRETACEOUS PERIOD	PALEOGENE PERIOD / NEOGENE PERIOD / QUATERNARY PERIOD

years ago and ruled for 100 million years. And we did it with our eyes. Eyes left, eyes right, eyes left, eyes right.

Oh, I'm starving! What do you mean *Have a bit of squid and calm down*? I can't. Use your eyes! There aren't any squid! They've all *squidaddled*!

I'm not a dolphin!

Not enough squid

ICHTHYOSAUR

TIME OF EXTINCTION	Mid-nineteenth century
SIZE	6 inches (15.4 centimeters) total length
AREA	Ogasawara Islands
FOOD	Fruit of trees
TYPE	Bird

The goats ate everything

This is the culprit.

Regrets?
If we'd still been able to fly, we wouldn't have been stuck on the ground.

The birds' name in Japanese, *mashiko*, means "a child of a monkey," since the birds' red faces made them look like Japanese monkeys. They lived on the ground and lowest branches, eating fruit and buds, and didn't fly farther up. The Ogasawara Islands had been almost uninhabited by humans until the nineteenth century. When humans settled there, bringing in livestock, the Bonin grosbeak lost their source of food to the goats. They were also attacked by cats, and rats ate their eggs. They seem to have died out quite quickly.

PRECAMBRIAN	PALEOZOIC ERA	MESOZOIC ERA	CENOZOIC ERA
	CAMBRIAN PERIOD / ORDOVICIAN PERIOD / SILURIAN PERIOD / DEVONIAN PERIOD / CARBONIFEROUS PERIOD / PERMIAN PERIOD	TRIASSIC PERIOD / JURASSIC PERIOD / CRETACEOUS PERIOD	PALEOGENE PERIOD / NEOGENE PERIOD / QUATERNARY PERIOD

Ladies and gentlemen. Good afternoon! My name in English is Bonin grosbeak—but my name in Japanese, Ogasawara mashiko, is far more elegant.

Until I became extinct toward the end of Japan's Edo period (1603–1867), my home was in the Ogasawara Islands, otherwise known as the Bonin Islands.

Long ago, there were no humans on the islands, and I had no enemies. I was fortunate—I could live simply by picking up the fruits that fell from the bushes and trees around me. I may be a bird, but I must confess I am not terribly keen on flying.

So, what happened? I'll tell you. The goats arrived!

From around 1830, human beings from various different places came to live on the islands. And they brought goats. And the goats ate absolutely everything there was on the ground. All I could do was stare down at the bare earth. And the bare earth just stared right back at me.

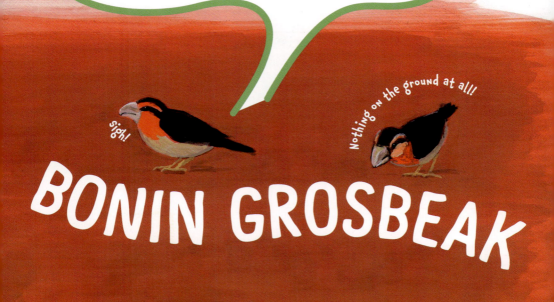

BONIN GROSBEAK

A: Not much room in this river!
B: So why don't you two get out and go somewhere else? Go on!
C: Can't! We're warming up ourselves in the sunshine.
A: We don't want to start walking about on the ground. These sail things on our backs always get in the way.
B: So you're just going to stay here in the river?
A & C: There's no other choice.
B: Why don't we all go to the sea?
A: Don't be silly!

What can we do?

Regrets?
If only we'd been smaller, things might have been easier.

The spinosaurus was one of the largest carnivorous dinosaurs. They were good swimmers; they lived in rivers and lakes and are thought to have caught fish by sweeping their long mouths from side to side through the water. The buoyancy of water let them grow big, but their size then made them bad at walking. When their numbers grew and the amount of available prey shrank, they would have found it difficult to move across land to other rivers. So they probably stayed where they were and died out there.

TIME OF EXTINCTION	Mid-Cretaceous period
SIZE	52 feet (15.8 meters) total length
AREA	Africa
FOOD	Fish
TYPE	Reptile

PRECAMBRIAN | PALEOZOIC ERA: CAMBRIAN PERIOD, ORDOVICIAN PERIOD, SILURIAN PERIOD, DEVONIAN PERIOD, CARBONIFEROUS PERIOD, PERMIAN PERIOD | MESOZOIC ERA: TRIASSIC PERIOD, JURASSIC PERIOD, **CRETACEOUS PERIOD** | CENOZOIC ERA: PALEOGENE PERIOD, NEOGENE PERIOD, QUATERNARY PERIOD

C: It's full of ichthyosaurs and plesiosaurs—very good swimmers.

B: You're right. That wouldn't suit us at all.

A: But . . . I'm so hungry!

C: Yeah, no fish here.

B: We've eaten them all.

A: Ha ha ha!

B: . . .

A: Sorry to laugh. It's not funny.

C: Maybe some tasty little dinosaurs might wander over for a drink of water.

B: Not with us here. We stand out a mile.

A, B & C: *Sigh*.

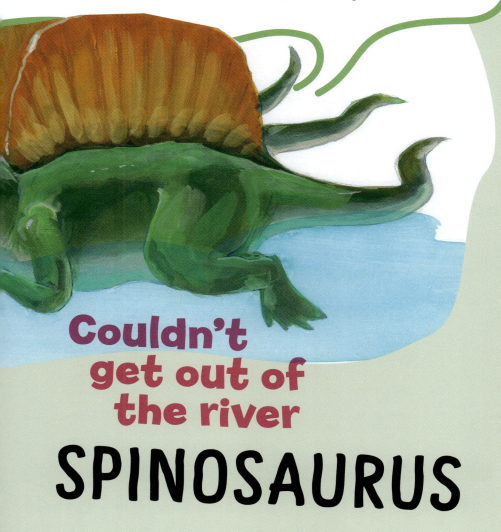

Couldn't get out of the river
SPINOSAURUS

A leisurely lunch

ARTHROPLEURA

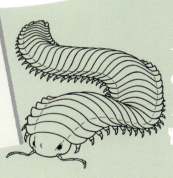

Regrets?
Maybe we should have been a bit smaller and quicker.

TIME OF EXTINCTION	End of Carboniferous period
SIZE	8 feet (2.4 meters) body length
AREA	North America
FOOD	Plants
TYPE	Myriapod

A close relative of today's centipedes and millipedes, the arthropleura is thought to have been the world's largest land arthropod. It grew in size during the Carboniferous period, when the climate was warm, oxygen levels were high, and it had no natural predators. By the early Permian period, the atmosphere had dried and the arthropleura population was falling. Meanwhile, newly evolved reptiles were growing in numbers, and it is thought that they hunted the arthropleura to extinction.

PRECAMBRIAN	PALEOZOIC ERA	MESOZOIC ERA	CENOZOIC ERA
	CAMBRIAN PERIOD / ORDOVICIAN PERIOD / SILURIAN PERIOD / DEVONIAN PERIOD / **CARBONIFEROUS PERIOD** / PERMIAN PERIOD	TRIASSIC PERIOD / JURASSIC PERIOD / CRETACEOUS PERIOD	PALEOGENE PERIOD / NEOGENE PERIOD / QUATERNARY PERIOD

A slow eater

Mmm . . . Feels funny . . . Is something nibbling at me? Ah well! Never mind that now. I'm famished. I'm hooked on these ferns. They're absolutely, like, wow!

Anyway, it was, I dunno, about three hundred million years ago—the air got very dry, and the forests we lived in shrank.

And about the same time lots of, like, lizardy little reptiles turned up. I thought they were cute at first, but then they all got together and starting eating me. It was a bit depressing, really.

I may look tough, but I'm no good at fighting and stuff like that. All I eat is leaves and things. I'm a bit heavy, to be honest, and on the slow side. I couldn't exactly run off and escape from the forest.

So when they saw me taking my time over my food, they all moved in and, like, gobbled me up. Hadn't even finished my lunch. . . .

The looks of a sparrow, the sense of a poultry chick. That's us! We had very few enemies on Stephens Island, and after we'd been there awhile, we found we could no longer fly.

Things were very peaceful on the island before the humans came.

Then one day a lighthouse appeared. And humans came to live there. They brought a cat with them—a single pregnant female cat. We'd never seen a cat before. We were excited. We thought it might be a new friend for us. We went right up to it. And before we knew what was happening, one of us was dead. After that, the cat came out hunting us almost every day. It had kittens, and they came hunting too. That cat family massacred us. We were wiped out completely.

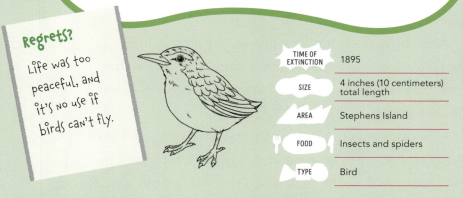

Regrets?
Life was too peaceful, and it's no use if birds can't fly.

TIME OF EXTINCTION	1895
SIZE	4 inches (10 centimeters) total length
AREA	Stephens Island
FOOD	Insects and spiders
TYPE	Bird

Having evolved in New Zealand, where it had no mammal predators, Lyall's wren had lost the ability to fly. It died out on the main islands when people and rats arrived. But it managed to survive on Stephens Island, where nobody lived. When a lighthouse was built on the island and the keepers brought a cat, the remaining population of Lyall's wrens was killed off. The species was registered for the first time in 1894 after a cat brought a dead bird back to the lighthouse.

PRECAMBRIAN	PALEOZOIC ERA						MESOZOIC ERA			CENOZOIC ERA		
	CAMBRIAN PERIOD	ORDOVICIAN PERIOD	SILURIAN PERIOD	DEVONIAN PERIOD	CARBONIFEROUS PERIOD	PERMIAN PERIOD	TRIASSIC PERIOD	JURASSIC PERIOD	CRETACEOUS PERIOD	PALEOGENE PERIOD	NEOGENE PERIOD	QUATERNARY PERIOD

Wiped out by a cat

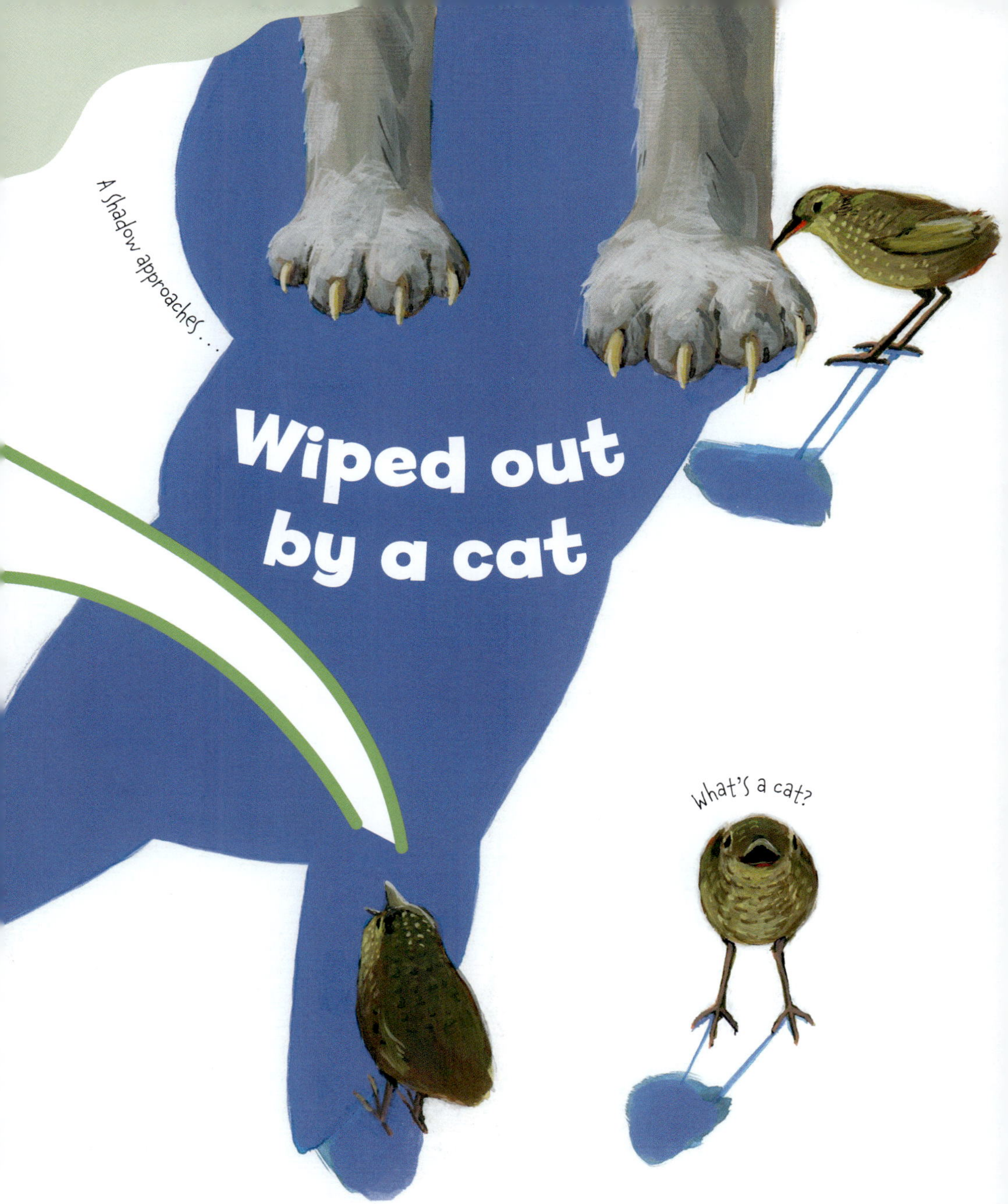

A shadow approaches . . .
What's a cat?

LYALL'S WREN

Burp. Sorry about that! I've got another twenty froglets waiting to come out of my mouth! We raise the little ones in our stomachs, you see. Things have been so dangerous recently, haven't they? That's why we swallow all our eggs after we lay them. We let the froglets out when they've grown up a bit, bless 'em. *Croak.* Excuse me! Here comes another. . . . There we are!

Anyway, it was illness that did us in. An epidemic came here to Australia from the Korean peninsula; chytridiomycosis, it was called. Killed us all off.

We breathe through our skin, us frogs. And this illness covered our skin in mold. All over! We couldn't breathe!

Makes you wonder why you bother, really. Swallowing all those children! What on earth was the point?

Regrets?

If our population had been spread over a wider area, we might not have all died out.

TIME OF EXTINCTION	1983
SIZE	1.4 inches (3.6 centimeters) total length
AREA	Australia
FOOD	Insects
TYPE	Amphibian

The Southern gastric-brooding frog reared its offspring inside its stomach. The mother swallowed her spawn and stopped eating while the spawn developed into tadpoles and then frogs. During this period, the mother's stomach secreted no gastric juices. Once the frogs had formed, they came back up out of the mother's mouth. There were not many of these frogs when they were first discovered, and their habitat range was limited to riversides between 1,100 to 2,600 feet above sea level. They were badly affected by dam construction and forestry operations, and seem to have been finished off by chytridiomycosis, an amphibian disease brought to the area by humans.

PRECAMBRIAN	PALEOZOIC ERA	MESOZOIC ERA	CENOZOIC ERA
	CAMBRIAN PERIOD / ORDOVICIAN PERIOD / SILURIAN PERIOD / DEVONIAN PERIOD / CARBONIFEROUS PERIOD / PERMIAN PERIOD	TRIASSIC PERIOD / JURASSIC PERIOD / CRETACEOUS PERIOD	PALEOGENE PERIOD / NEOGENE PERIOD / QUATERNARY PERIOD

SOUTHERN GASTRIC-BROODING FROG

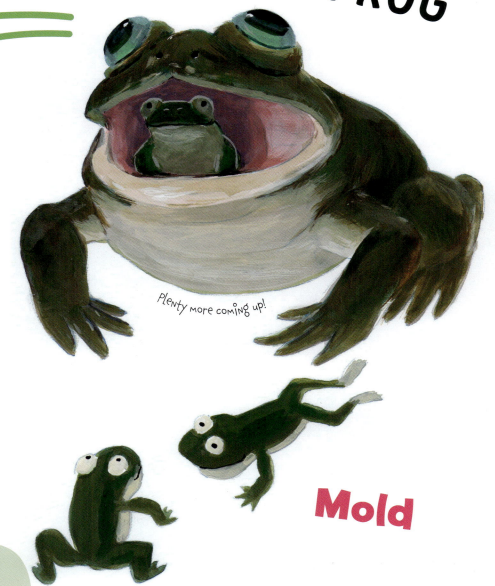

Plenty more coming up!

Mold

Like what you see? Quite something, huh? It's my legs that do it, really—they're over six feet long! I was the biggest land animal in New Zealand. Beautiful and invincible.

So I ditched my wings. Why keep them? I never had to escape from any enemy. All I had to do was walk gracefully around, eating leaves off the trees. What a wonderful time that was!

But then humans came. They wanted meat and they started hunting us. Their method was horrifying!

We had no teeth, so we ate pebbles to help break up the food in our stomachs. When the humans noticed that, they started heating up little stones in their fires. When the stones were scorching hot, they put them out for us to eat. I'll never forgive them for that!

Regrets?
We should have checked whether the stones were hot before we swallowed them.

TIME OF EXTINCTION	Approximately sixteenth century
SIZE	12 feet (3.6 meters) tall
AREA	New Zealand
FOOD	Leaves and small branches
TYPE	Bird

New Zealand had no mammals except bats, so birds had no mammal predators, and many species evolved that could not fly. These included the moas. The giant moa was, as far as we know, the tallest bird ever to have existed. It weighed 500 pounds and reigned supreme, with no rivals at all. But when humans arrived in the ninth and tenth centuries, they began to hunt the giant moa for its meat, which eventually led to its extinction.

PRECAMBRIAN | PALEOZOIC ERA (CAMBRIAN PERIOD, ORDOVICIAN PERIOD, SILURIAN PERIOD, DEVONIAN PERIOD, CARBONIFEROUS PERIOD, PERMIAN PERIOD) | MESOZOIC ERA (TRIASSIC PERIOD, JURASSIC PERIOD, CRETACEOUS PERIOD) | CENOZOIC ERA (PALEOGENE PERIOD, NEOGENE PERIOD, QUATERNARY PERIOD)

GIANT MOA

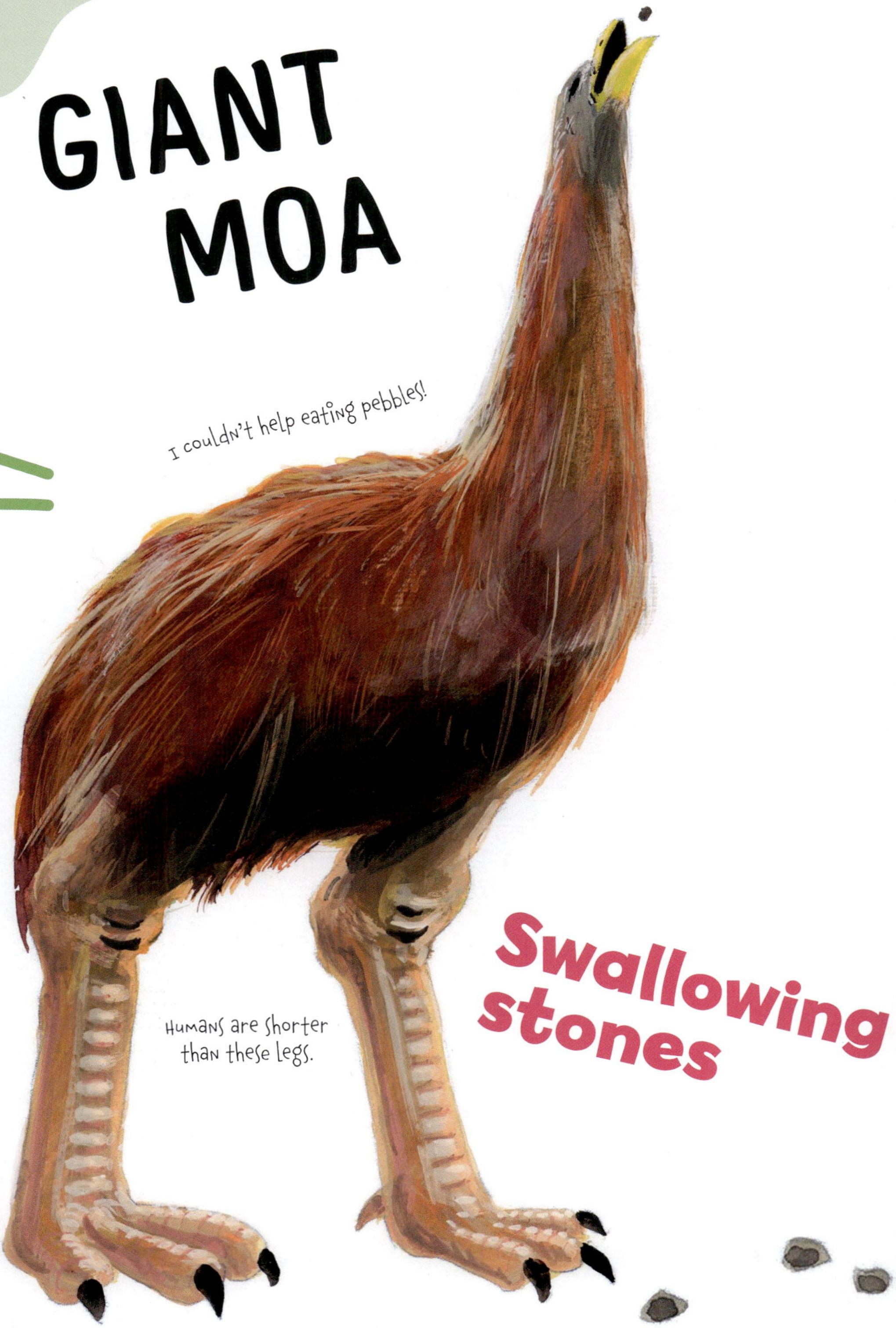
I couldn't help eating pebbles!
Humans are shorter than these legs.

Swallowing stones

(Umm . . .) (. . . What?) (I just wondered if something might be eating me. . . .) (Ah, yes. That's right.) (Oh. No!) (Gotta fight!) (Can't.) (Why not?) (Got no weapons.) (That's true.) (No teeth.) (No mouth.) (No eyes.) (No legs.) (No shell.) (Too soft.) (Exposed.) (But we managed

As soft as the day it was born

Regrets?

(I wish we'd been tougher, even if it had meant hurting someone.)

It seems that in the Ediacaran period, at the end of the Precambrian era, animals produced energy through exposure to sunlight, like plants do through photosynthesis, and they absorbed nutrients from seawater. They had no mouth, eyes, or fins, and their bodies were very soft. Very few fossils remain. The largest of these creatures were dickinsonia. They were presumably living a peaceful existence when new predator species came onto the scene—with eyes, mouths, and fins—and ate them all up.

TIME OF EXTINCTION	Precambrian
SIZE	3 feet (0.9 meter) total length
AREA	Australia
FOOD	Photosynthesis
TYPE	Ediacaran biota

to live.) (We did back then.) (But at some point things changed.) (The strong ate the weak.) (A hierarchy developed.) (We were the type that got eaten.) (We were unlucky.) (That's all there was to it.)

Too soft

Gobbled up
So many mysteries

DICKINSONIA

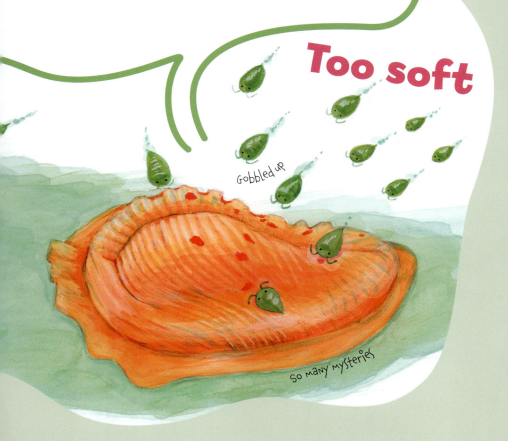

I'm not a rat! I'm a pig-footed bandicoot—a marsupial, like a kangaroo, only much smaller. I've got a pouch near my tummy to carry my children in, and I only eat grass.

We used to live in the Australian grassland, but then Aboriginal humans came into our habitat, and so we moved out into the desert. Our numbers fell, but we managed to survive, running about looking for food.

But then, about three hundred years ago, European humans came to Australia, and life really changed. They wanted bigger farms to keep cattle and sheep, and they released rabbits and foxes into the bush so that they could go hunting and shooting. It was terrible for us. The rabbits ate all the grass, and the foxes attacked us. Should have given them a good punch, kangaroo-style.

Regrets?
We should have eaten insects and fruit instead of just grass.

TIME OF EXTINCTION	1901
SIZE	10 inches (25.4 centimeters) body length
AREA	Australia
FOOD	Grass
TYPE	Mammal

The pig-footed bandicoot's main food was grass, for which its long intestine was well-suited. It used to run around the grassland on its spindly legs, but it was gradually forced out into the desert by encroaching humans. When Europeans later introduced rabbits and foxes, the rabbits took the bandicoots' nesting sites and food, and the foxes hunted them out of existence.

PRECAMBRIAN	PALEOZOIC ERA	MESOZOIC ERA	CENOZOIC ERA
	CAMBRIAN PERIOD / ORDOVICIAN PERIOD / SILURIAN PERIOD / DEVONIAN PERIOD / CARBONIFEROUS PERIOD / PERMIAN PERIOD	TRIASSIC PERIOD / JURASSIC PERIOD / CRETACEOUS PERIOD	PALEOGENE PERIOD / NEOGENE PERIOD / QUATERNARY PERIOD

Attacked by foxes

Front paws like a pig's trotters and back paws like a horse's hooves

PIG-FOOTED BANDICOOT

Canina! Why have you come back? We promised we wouldn't meet again! And now for some reason, the hunters are after me. It's dangerous. You must go home. Quickly!

Of course, I'm pleased you were thinking about me. But that's not the point. . . .

There's this terrible illness going round. Wolves get a fever, sneezing, runny nose. They start barking and howling uncontrollably, and then they just die!

I want to believe it's not your fault! But ever since Europeans and Americans started bringing their pets to Japan, a lot of my friends have been dying. It's like there's some kind of major biohazard out there.

So for both our sakes, we've got to end it. You see that, don't you? Hey! Your nose is running. It's getting all over the place. Stop it! Stop rubbing yourself against me like that. Please?

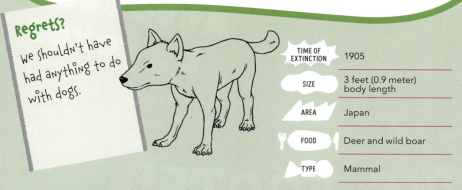

Regrets?
We shouldn't have had anything to do with dogs.

TIME OF EXTINCTION	1905
SIZE	3 feet (0.9 meter) body length
AREA	Japan
FOOD	Deer and wild boar
TYPE	Mammal

In Japan's Meiji period (1868–1912), a lot of foreigners came to live there. Their pet dogs brought distemper and rabies viruses. In those days, dogs were left to roam about as they liked, so it didn't take long for the viruses to spread from the westerners' pet dogs to Japanese breeds, then to wolves living near towns and villages, and finally to wolves in the mountains. As a result, just thirty-seven years after the start of the Meiji period, the Japanese wolf was extinct.

JAPANESE WOLF

Infected by dogs

couldn't beat the virus

But the dogs didn't die out...

Hold on, mister! It weren't me that ate your bloomin' sheep! Just 'cause I'm called a wolf, that don't mean nothin'. It's only a name! Understood?

We used to be all over Australia and other places, too, but you humans forced us out, and in the end the only place we was left was Tasmania. Then what happens? There we are, living honest

The dogs are enjoying themselves.

Regrets?
Maybe we should have sucked up to humans like dogs do.

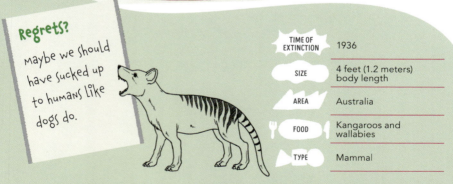

TIME OF EXTINCTION	1936
SIZE	4 feet (1.2 meters) body length
AREA	Australia
FOOD	Kangaroos and wallabies
TYPE	Mammal

Tasmanian wolves lived all over Australia and New Guinea, but they died out in most places ten thousand years ago. That was because they had lost their food and habitat after humans brought dogs into their areas. A small population managed to survive in Tasmania, where no dogs had been introduced. However, when Europeans settled in Tasmania in the nineteenth century, the Tasmanian wolves were hunted down because they were thought to be a threat to livestock. A reward was offered to anybody who killed one. Soon they were entirely extinct.

PRECAMBRIAN	PALEOZOIC ERA						MESOZOIC ERA			CENOZOIC ERA		
	CAMBRIAN PERIOD	ORDOVICIAN PERIOD	SILURIAN PERIOD	DEVONIAN PERIOD	CARBONIFEROUS PERIOD	PERMIAN PERIOD	TRIASSIC PERIOD	JURASSIC PERIOD	CRETACEOUS PERIOD	PALEOGENE PERIOD	NEOGENE PERIOD	QUATERNARY PERIOD

lives, minding our own business, when along you come again and start accusing us of eating your sheep—and then beat us to a pulp. Is that fair? I don't think so!

So, look, I'm telling you it weren't me! It were dogs. You brought them here and then you let them go wild. And now they eat your sheep! Oy! Mutt! All that wagging won't fool me! You're a nasty piece of work, mate!

TASMANIAN WOLF

Suffered for its name

Took the blame for dogs' crimes

Will someone please tell me what is going on?! Where on earth are my pretty eggs? Somebody must have taken them . . . again! It's those ghastly mammals! To think that a short while ago they were all just little things running around our feet. They're so big now! And they have the nerve to be quicker than we are.

Can you imagine doing anything so awful? You see some eggs all nicely laid together on the ground and then you just take them away and eat them! So ungracious! Why don't they become vegetarian, like me? I mean, really!

With those terrifying dinosaurs gone, I thought we birds could really come into our own. But now the mammals have taken over—stolen our rightful crown. It's so utterly galling!

Regrets? Maybe if we'd been smarter about where to put our nests.

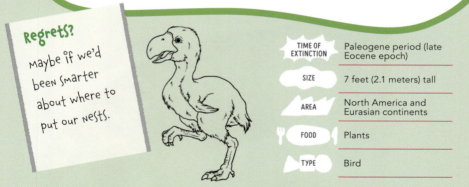

TIME OF EXTINCTION	Paleogene period (late Eocene epoch)
SIZE	7 feet (2.1 meters) tall
AREA	North America and Eurasian continents
FOOD	Plants
TYPE	Bird

Diatryma was a large flightless bird that stood seven feet tall, with a heavy head and beak that would have prevented it from running fast. Once suspected to be carnivorous, it is now thought to have had a diet of tree fruits instead. Diatrymas evolved to be larger after the extinction of the dinosaurs but were later preyed on by carnivorous mammals, which had also gotten bigger. This, together with losses to predators of eggs and chicks, is thought to have driven them to extinction.

PRECAMBRIAN	PALEOZOIC ERA	MESOZOIC ERA	CENOZOIC ERA
	CAMBRIAN PERIOD / ORDOVICIAN PERIOD / SILURIAN PERIOD / DEVONIAN PERIOD / CARBONIFEROUS PERIOD / PERMIAN PERIOD	TRIASSIC PERIOD / JURASSIC PERIOD / CRETACEOUS PERIOD	**PALEOGENE PERIOD** / NEOGENE PERIOD / QUATERNARY PERIOD

DIATRYMA

Didn't look after its eggs

where have my eggs gone?!

Who called the shots in South America a million years ago? That'll be me, honey. And I lasted a long time! The biggest, strongest creature in the land. Megatherium—Big Meg. Twenty feet long. Three tons of fun. Just take a look at my claws! A match for a saber-toothed tiger* any day of the week. Pleased to make your acquaintance.

Huh? You laughing? I may be a sloth, but I am *not at all* like the sloths of today. I walked the ground, tearing branches from the trees, devouring their leaves. And my fur was thick, and my bones were like rods of iron—no bite could bother me at all.

So why did I go extinct? I was hunted by humans. They attacked me in groups. They saw I was a bit slow and took advantage. Yeah. It was my sloth nature. . . .

But to be killed off by those teeny little humans! I must have been losing my touch.

*p. 72

Regrets?
If I'd climbed trees or run fast, I might have survived.

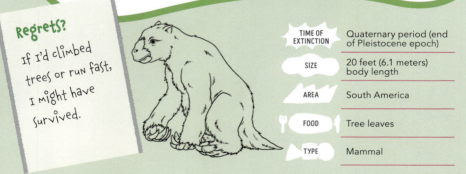

TIME OF EXTINCTION	Quaternary period (end of Pleistocene epoch)
SIZE	20 feet (6.1 meters) body length
AREA	South America
FOOD	Tree leaves
TYPE	Mammal

The megatherium was the largest species of giant sloth and the last to develop. It lived in South America, where it had no effective competitor or predator. Until three million years ago, South America was a totally separate continent; because there were no powerful carnivores there, like dogs or cats, the giant sloths could grow big, even though they were so slow. They died out ten thousand years ago, after groups of humans started attacking them with weapons.

PRECAMBRIAN | PALEOZOIC ERA (CAMBRIAN PERIOD, ORDOVICIAN PERIOD, SILURIAN PERIOD, DEVONIAN PERIOD, CARBONIFEROUS PERIOD, PERMIAN PERIOD) | MESOZOIC ERA (TRIASSIC PERIOD, JURASSIC PERIOD, CRETACEOUS PERIOD) | CENOZOIC ERA (PALEOGENE PERIOD, NEOGENE PERIOD, **QUATERNARY PERIOD**)

MEGATHERIUM

No enemies

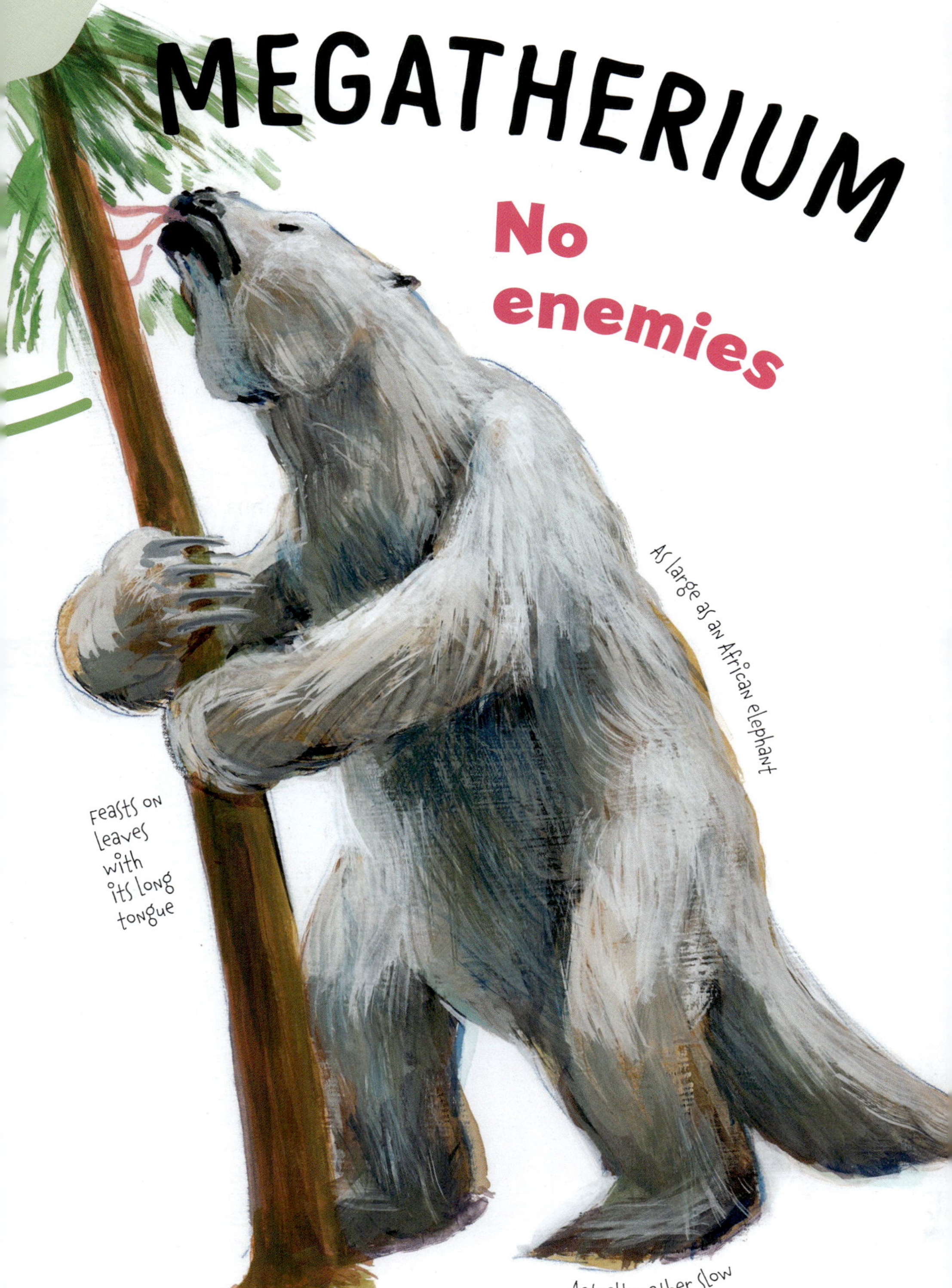
As large as an African elephant
Feasts on leaves with its long tongue
Actually rather slow

If you wanna be left standing

You can't stick to the trends

Too much glam forever, then one day it ends. . . .

PART 2
Just Too Extra

I went to extremes.

Animals evolve quickly.
Whether they are evolving in a way that will ultimately help them, nobody knows.
But if things are taken too far, there's a good chance that life may get difficult.

Hello! I'm a platybelodon, a kind of elephant. What's wrong? You staring at my chin? I know, it sticks out a long way. But I swear I'm an elephant. The genuine article.

These flat shovel-like teeth are for getting food—scooping up roots, snapping off branches, stripping off bark. Just the thing for the job, you may think. Well, actually, no. These teeth were much too heavy. My head

Regrets?

It was only my nose that had to get longer. . . .

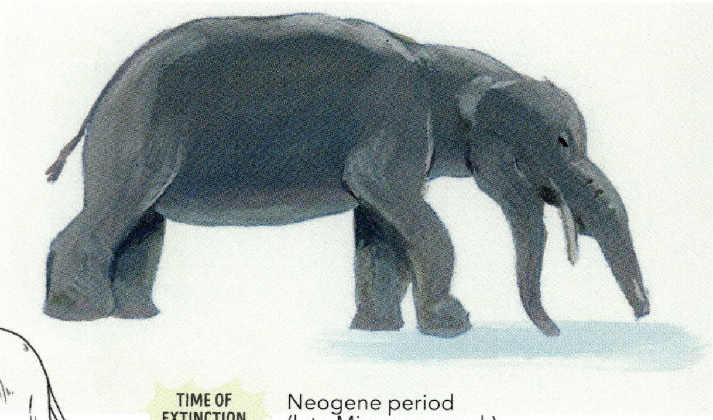

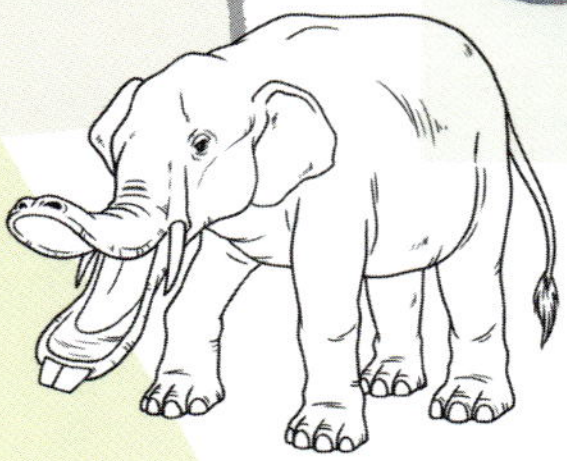

TIME OF EXTINCTION	Neogene period (late Miocene epoch)
SIZE	7 feet (2.1 meters) shoulder height
AREA	Africa, Eurasian continent, North America
FOOD	Grass and bark
TYPE	Mammal

As elephants' ancestors grew bigger, their noses and upper lips combined and grew longer. This enabled them to drink water without crouching down. The platybelodon developed not just a long nose but a long lower jaw as well, and at the end of the jaw were tusks that resembled buck teeth. Today, only the elephant's nose is long, while their upper front teeth are their two tusks.

PRECAMBRIAN	PALEOZOIC ERA						MESOZOIC ERA			CENOZOIC ERA		
	CAMBRIAN PERIOD	ORDOVICIAN PERIOD	SILURIAN PERIOD	DEVONIAN PERIOD	CARBONIFEROUS PERIOD	PERMIAN PERIOD	TRIASSIC PERIOD	JURASSIC PERIOD	CRETACEOUS PERIOD	PALEOGENE PERIOD	NEOGENE PERIOD	QUATERNARY PERIOD

was big enough anyway, and so trying to use this jaw to get roots out of the ground was real tough work. Made it difficult to chew too. Imagine trying to eat with weights hanging from your chin. Terrible, right?

I wore myself out just eating. I had no children. That was that.

Chin too heavy

PLATYBELODON

I'm not making a funny face.

I know they get in the way. But I don't want to get rid of them. I can't. Every tooth is a monument to a past fight. They weren't like this when I was small. I didn't have these whorls of teeth then. But as I grew, they gradually developed too. First one whorl, then another, and another. New teeth formed on the outside while the older teeth got wrapped around inside.

How big are they going to get? What about ulcers?

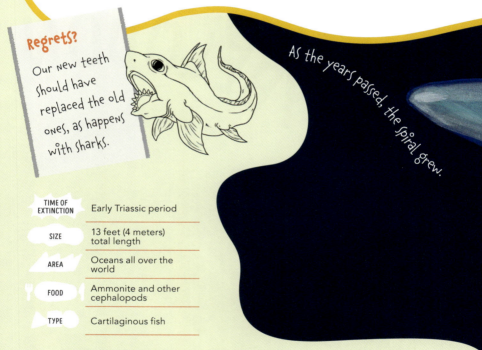

Regrets?
Our new teeth should have replaced the old ones, as happens with sharks.

As the years passed, the spiral grew.

TIME OF EXTINCTION	Early Triassic period
SIZE	13 feet (4 meters) total length
AREA	Oceans all over the world
FOOD	Ammonite and other cephalopods
TYPE	Cartilaginous fish

A supposed relative of sharks and rays, this strange creature called the helicoprion had no teeth at all on its upper jaw but developed a spiral of teeth on its lower jaw, adding new teeth without losing older ones. The advantage of retaining old teeth is not known for certain, but one theory is that the sharp whorl of teeth was perfect for catching ammonites and other slippery cephalopods. But when the cephalopod-eating ichthyosaur arrived, the helicoprion disappeared, as if it had simply been replaced.

PRECAMBRIAN	PALEOZOIC ERA						MESOZOIC ERA			CENOZOIC ERA		
	CAMBRIAN PERIOD	ORDOVICIAN PERIOD	SILURIAN PERIOD	DEVONIAN PERIOD	CARBONIFEROUS PERIOD	PERMIAN PERIOD	TRIASSIC PERIOD	JURASSIC PERIOD	CRETACEOUS PERIOD	PALEOGENE PERIOD	NEOGENE PERIOD	QUATERNARY PERIOD

Worries like these were always in the back of my mind.

After a while, I began to feel sure that this was a trial—an ordeal to make me stronger. These teeth helped us eat hard-shelled ammonites. That was how we had survived for sixty million years.

But then the ichthyosaurs* arrived. With their long, narrow mouths, they were very quick to catch their prey, and we found ourselves with much less food. Eventually, we died out completely.

*p. 8

Teeth didn't come out

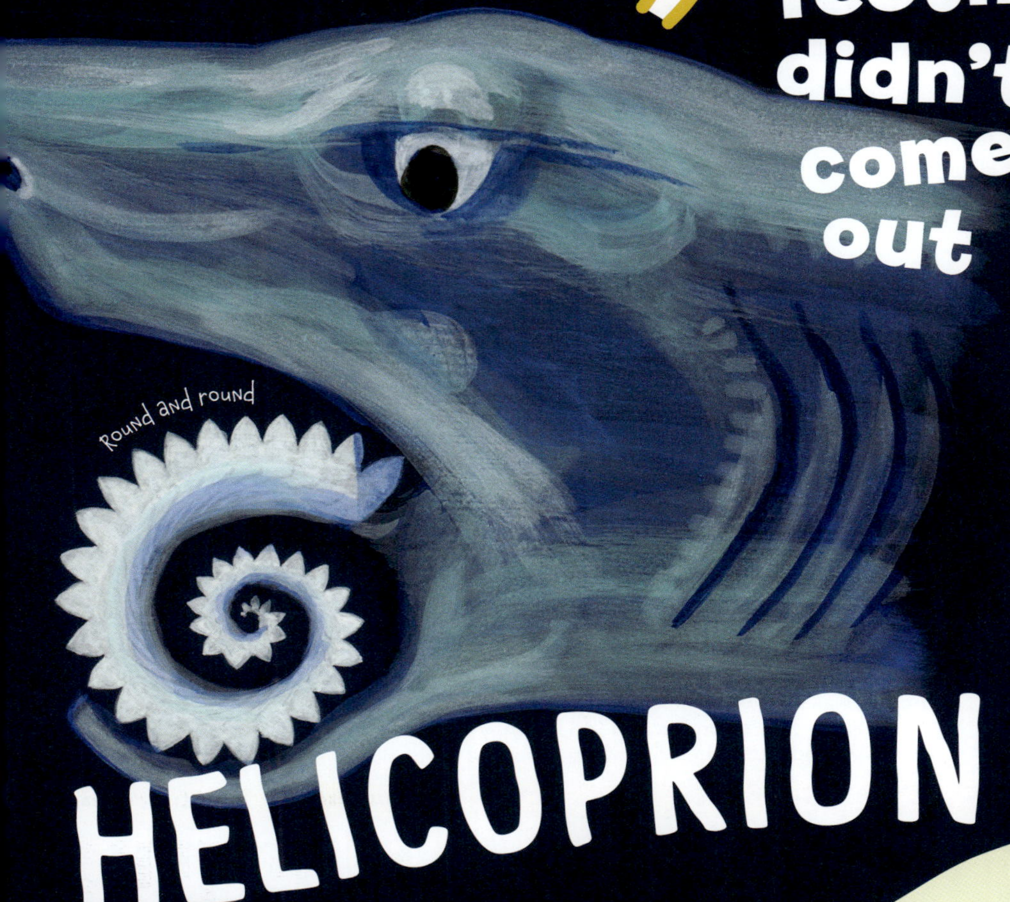
Round and round

HELICOPRION

Yoo-hoo! I'm a pigeon! Got plenty of those, you say? Well, when we were around, there were a lot more!

At one time there were five billion of us. When we took to the sky, there were so many of us that we blocked out the sun. The sound was so loud that people couldn't hear each other speak! After we'd gone, our droppings would lie on the ground as deep as snow. Like something from a fairy-tale land!

Regrets?
maybe we wouldn't have been shot if we'd flown in smaller, less conspicuous groups.

I'm actually pretty muscular.

TIME OF EXTINCTION	1914
SIZE	16 inches (40.6 centimeters) total length
AREA	North America
FOOD	Seeds and fruit
TYPE	Bird

Passenger pigeons were thought to have had larger populations than any other bird in history. The individual birds lived a long time and protected themselves from natural predators (like eagles) by forming huge flocks. But their reproductive capacity was low, with only one egg being laid per female per year. If they stayed in one place, they'd run out of food, so they had to keep moving. But European settlers waited along their flyways and hunted them all.

PRECAMBRIAN | PALEOZOIC ERA (CAMBRIAN PERIOD, ORDOVICIAN PERIOD, SILURIAN PERIOD, DEVONIAN PERIOD, CARBONIFEROUS PERIOD, PERMIAN PERIOD) | MESOZOIC ERA (TRIASSIC PERIOD, JURASSIC PERIOD, CRETACEOUS PERIOD) | CENOZOIC ERA (PALEOGENE PERIOD, NEOGENE PERIOD, QUATERNARY PERIOD)

Every year, we'd fly between Canada and Mexico looking for food. Then, one day, humans started firing guns at us. *Bang, bang, bang!* There were so many of us that they didn't even have to aim—any shot would hit several birds at once. They'd shoot as many as two hundred thousand a day, hunting us for our meat and feathers.

There may well have been too many of us, but the humans went too far!

PASSENGER PIGEON

Too many

can't cope with that crowd!

No, I can't! It's impossible! I can't suddenly bend myself. Look at my shell! It's nearly thirty-three feet long.

What? *Make it smaller*? How on earth am I going to do that? If I don't keep all the fluid inside my shell, my balance is thrown off. But I know what you mean. My shell is heavy and makes me very slow. I can't change direction quickly enough.

We have a relative called nautilus* with a spiral shell—very compact. To be honest, I envy him.

*p. 136

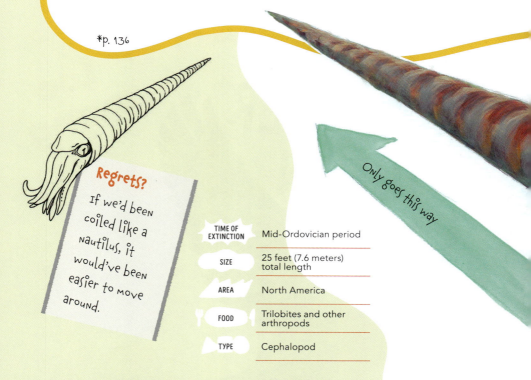

Regrets?
If we'd been coiled like a nautilus, it would've been easier to move around.

Only goes this way

TIME OF EXTINCTION	Mid-Ordovician period
SIZE	25 feet (7.6 meters) total length
AREA	North America
FOOD	Trilobites and other arthropods
TYPE	Cephalopod

The cameroceras's shell was big, but its body only took up one-sixth of the space inside. The remainder was divided into small segments. The cameroceras was able to move up and down in the water by adjusting the amount of fluid held in these segments. Thought to have been the largest animal in the Ordovician period, it had no major natural enemies. The species probably died out because its members grew too big and couldn't move easily. One theory is that they became stuck on the seabed.

PRECAMBRIAN	PALEOZOIC ERA						MESOZOIC ERA			CENOZOIC ERA		
	CAMBRIAN PERIOD	ORDOVICIAN PERIOD	SILURIAN PERIOD	DEVONIAN PERIOD	CARBONIFEROUS PERIOD	PERMIAN PERIOD	TRIASSIC PERIOD	JURASSIC PERIOD	CRETACEOUS PERIOD	PALEOGENE PERIOD	NEOGENE PERIOD	QUATERNARY PERIOD

But don't get me wrong. I'm proud to be what I am—a no-nonsense guy, straight as an arrow. My shell just means I have to think more in advance when I'm trying catch some prey. Because if we're going for one, and at the last moment it decides, *Oh, I'll go this way*, we can't change course and—whoosh—we just go sailing straight past, no choice. Whoosh!

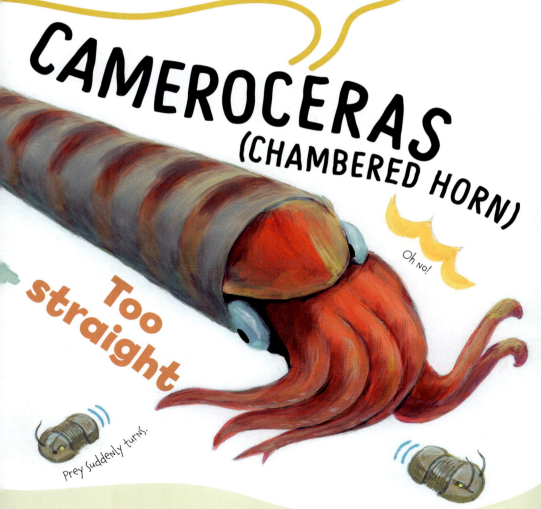

CAMEROCERAS (CHAMBERED HORN)

Oh no!

Too straight

Prey suddenly turns.

Hey, you! I know what you're thinking . . . but it's okay. You can think what you like! If my shell reminds you of a pile of doo-doo, that's fine by me.

I know I don't look that great, but the strange thing is, I'm part of the once-mighty ammonite dynasty. In fact, I evolved just as that ancient clan was petering out, a kind of oddball relation who turned up at the end of the party.

Still, inside this strange shell I'm pretty much like any other ammonite you care to mention.

And I suppose till I arrived, there'd been nothing in the family but those smart curly shells for 350 million years, so maybe it was time for a design change. But in my case, it didn't quite work out. Ha ha!

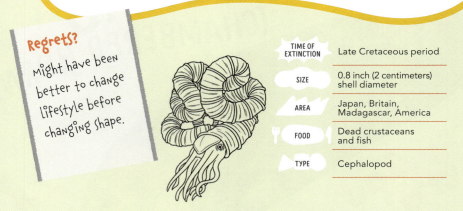

Regrets?
Might have been better to change lifestyle before changing shape.

TIME OF EXTINCTION	Late Cretaceous period
SIZE	0.8 inch (2 centimeters) shell diameter
AREA	Japan, Britain, Madagascar, America
FOOD	Dead crustaceans and fish
TYPE	Cephalopod

Ammonites flourished for 350 million years, from the Paleozoic era to the Mesozoic era. But by the Cretaceous period at the end of the Mesozoic era, their numbers had fallen greatly. That's when the nipponites appeared. They'd evolved a shell that coiled very differently to those of any previous ammonites, but it doesn't seem to have helped them much in life, and they died out within a very short period.

In a tangle

Total confusion

Normally an ammonite shell is like this.

Evolution took a turn that's a mystery even to me.

NIPPONITES

My heart is broken! Will it never mend? Will the dark clouds of sadness never lift?

Long ago we used to roam widely over grassland in South Africa. Then, about thirty-five thousand years ago, trees started to appear on the grassland, and we lost a lot of our habitat.

So we had to change our lifestyle. We started living in much smaller areas in herds of five or six.

Then humans came, looking for diamonds and gold. No sooner had they seen us than they started to hunt us.

I dare say our bluish coats must have struck them as unusual. Those of us who were killed were sold as stuffed animals, or used to make human coats.

Two hundred years ago, the last of us died, and with that, we disappeared from the world.

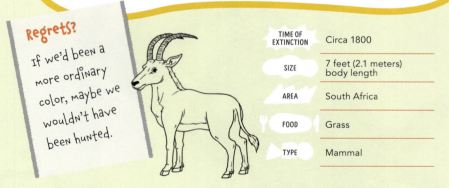

Regrets?
If we'd been a more ordinary color, maybe we wouldn't have been hunted.

TIME OF EXTINCTION	Circa 1800
SIZE	7 feet (2.1 meters) body length
AREA	South Africa
FOOD	Grass
TYPE	Mammal

Blue is an extremely unusual color for a mammal's fur. However, the exact shade of the living bluebuck is not known, because all museum specimens having faded to gray. Bluebuck numbers were already low by the time they were discovered by humans, and after 120 years of being hunted for their beautiful coats, the species died out altogether. The bluebuck is thought to have been the first large animal in Africa to have been wiped out by humans.

PRECAMBRIAN	PALEOZOIC ERA						MESOZOIC ERA			CENOZOIC ERA		
	CAMBRIAN PERIOD	ORDOVICIAN PERIOD	SILURIAN PERIOD	DEVONIAN PERIOD	CARBONIFEROUS PERIOD	PERMIAN PERIOD	TRIASSIC PERIOD	JURASSIC PERIOD	CRETACEOUS PERIOD	PALEOGENE PERIOD	NEOGENE PERIOD	QUATERNARY PERIOD

Too beautiful

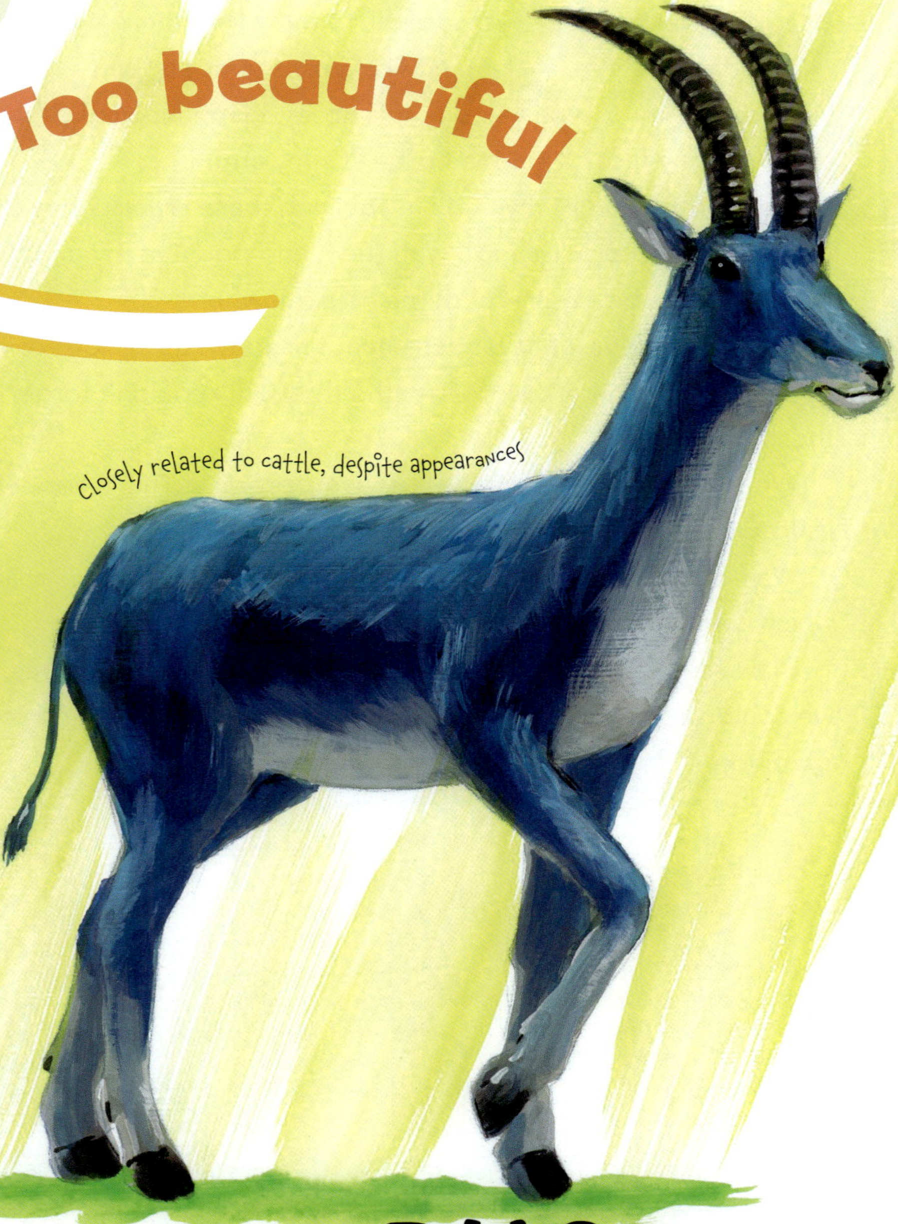
closely related to cattle, despite appearances

BLUEBUCK

Well, let me see . . . first of all, I simply love these eyes—five of them, sticking up like mushrooms so I can see backward! Then . . . oh yes, see this hosey, elephant-trunky thing in front of my face? It's not a nose—it's my arm!

Now, at the end of my arm I'm sporting these crablike pincers! Very practical. I pick up food with them and pop it in my mouth. My mouth is a bit lower—underneath somewhere . . .

And then, oh yes! I have these neat fins down both sides of my body, and gills there, too, to breathe through! I couldn't forget those, could I?!

What else? Ah yes, my tail—just like a prawn's! That's about it, I suppose.

Wait! I nearly forgot! I've got lots of warty little legs underneath, which come in handy for slithering around on the seafloor!

But even with all these fashionable accessories and features, we couldn't really cope when the environment changed, and so we died.

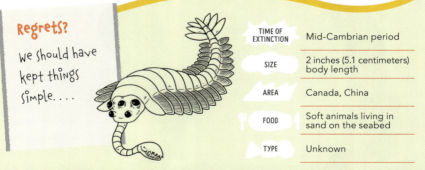

Regrets?
We should have kept things simple. . . .

TIME OF EXTINCTION	Mid-Cambrian period
SIZE	2 inches (5.1 centimeters) body length
AREA	Canada, China
FOOD	Soft animals living in sand on the seabed
TYPE	Unknown

When a diagram of an opabinia was first shown at a conference, the audience burst into laughter—many biologists didn't believe it was possible. The combination of features—hose and pincers, five eyes, multiple fins and legs—makes it entirely unique. The fact that no other animal like it has ever been discovered suggests that these kinds of "optional extras" were not helpful in terms of survival.

OPABINIA

Too much ornament

Its prey was pretty odd too!

Hi there! Hey . . . why the long face? Want to go for something to eat? How about some nice fresh grass?

That takes me back! It's the kind of line I used with my love, Philly!

We had the same ancestor as horses originally. Then, six thousand years ago, humans started interfering. Those of us that got on well with them became horses, and those that didn't just stayed in the wild, as tarpans.

From then on, we lived separate lives—till about two hundred years ago. The number of humans was increasing, and they were taking up more land, so our living space was shrinking. I found myself near a human's meadow, and then . . . it happened. Like a bolt of lightning. I saw Philly in the meadow. *This is my destiny*, I thought.

I galloped over and started chatting her up. I managed to get her to come with me out of the meadow. We had a lot of foals together, and as the generations came and went, all the tarpans became more and more like horses. In the end, there was no difference at all. We'd gone extinct—in the name of love.

Regrets?

We should have steered clear of humans.

TIME OF EXTINCTION	1909
SIZE	4 feet (1.2 meters) shoulder height
AREA	Europe
FOOD	Grass
TYPE	Mammal

Humans started keeping tarpans as livestock about six thousand years ago. At first, they were just a source of meat, but when the humans realized their domesticated horses could run fast carrying them on their backs, the horses became more important. Tarpans remained wild, but as the prairies shrank, they moved closer to the meadows, where the horses were kept. Some were shot by humans and some interbred with domestic horses, and eventually, they became extinct.

PRECAMBRIAN | PALEOZOIC ERA (CAMBRIAN PERIOD, ORDOVICIAN PERIOD, SILURIAN PERIOD, DEVONIAN PERIOD, CARBONIFEROUS PERIOD, PERMIAN PERIOD) | MESOZOIC ERA (TRIASSIC PERIOD, JURASSIC PERIOD, CRETACEOUS PERIOD) | CENOZOIC ERA (PALEOGENE PERIOD, NEOGENE PERIOD, QUATERNARY PERIOD)

A love affair with a horse

Furious meadow owner →

Philly, who stole his heart ↘

Runaway lovers

TARPAN

IRISH ELK

severe calcium deficiency

Regrets?
We should have built up our calcium somehow—eating eggshells, maybe!

The Irish elk's antlers were nearly ten feet wide and weighed a hundred pounds. This would have been awkward when drinking water and eating grass. On top of that, they grew new antlers every year, which required large quantities of calcium and phosphorous. It is thought that when forests shrank during the late Pleistocene period, Irish elks were unable to replenish the nutrients absorbed by their antlers, so their bones atrophied and they died out.

TIME OF EXTINCTION	Quaternary period (end of Pleistocene epoch)
SIZE	7 feet (2.1 meters) shoulder height
AREA	Eurasian continent
FOOD	Plants
TYPE	Mammal

PRECAMBRIAN | PALEOZOIC ERA (CAMBRIAN PERIOD, ORDOVICIAN PERIOD, SILURIAN PERIOD, DEVONIAN PERIOD, CARBONIFEROUS PERIOD, PERMIAN PERIOD) | MESOZOIC ERA (TRIASSIC PERIOD, JURASSIC PERIOD, CRETACEOUS PERIOD) | CENOZOIC ERA (PALEOGENE PERIOD, **NEOGENE PERIOD**, **QUATERNARY PERIOD**)

Antlers took all nutrients

Females had no antlers.

Argh! *Pant, pant.* Who would have thought such a thing could happen? Ugh! My antlers taking all my calcium?!

I had to fight other stags to win the affections of my doe. So I wanted my antlers to grow. *Be stronger, harder, bigger!*

But . . . they grew much faster than I had ever imagined.

All the nutrition in my body went straight to my antlers, while my bones grew thin and weak. The final blow came when the forest began to shrink, so there wasn't enough food. My bones are fragile now. I have to be very careful moving around.

Agh! I never knew the meaning of "despair" until now. I don't know why, but . . . I'm feeling very sleepy. . . . Please release me . . . quickly . . . from these antlers!

Uh-huh? So you'd like to know why I became extinct? Well, to put it very simply, I'd say the basic reason was that the shape of my beak was too specific.

Thirty-two species of Hawaiian honeycreeper have been identified, but each evolved in such a way that they never competed with others. Members of each species feed on very particular types of food, using the specialized length and shape of their beaks. My long beak meant that I had exclusive access to the rose apple's nectar.

But with the arrival of humans, the number of rose apple plants fell sharply, and as a result we became extinct. . . .

Regrets?
I'd say it's dangerous to rely too heavily on one thing. . . .

TIME OF EXTINCTION	1940
SIZE	6 inches (15.2 centimeters) total length
AREA	Hawaiian Islands
FOOD	Nectar and insects
TYPE	Bird

Different types of Hawaiian honeycreeper coexisted in the Hawaiian archipelago by eating different things. The bow-beaked honeycreeper developed its long curved beak to reach nectar inside long narrow flowers and insects deep inside trees. But specialist creatures find it difficult to cope with environmental change. Settlement by humans led to forests being cut down and replaced by fields, and the bird soon disappeared.

BOW-BEAKED HAWAIIAN HONEYCREEPER

Beak too specialized

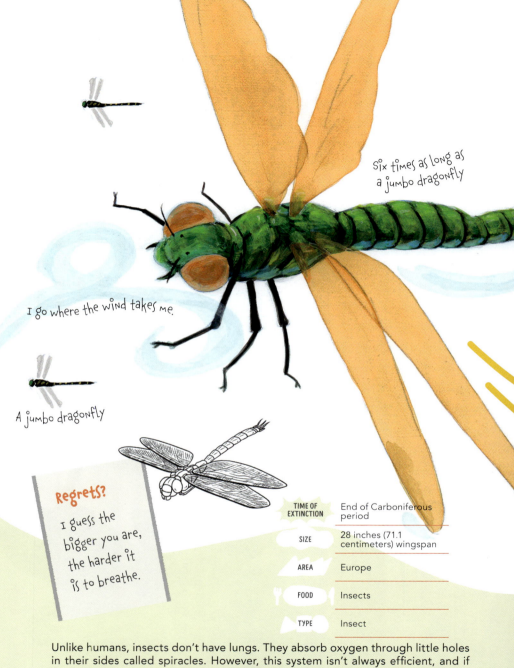

Six times as long as a jumbo dragonfly

I go where the wind takes me.

A jumbo dragonfly

Regrets?

I guess the bigger you are, the harder it is to breathe.

TIME OF EXTINCTION		End of Carboniferous period
SIZE		28 inches (71.1 centimeters) wingspan
AREA		Europe
FOOD		Insects
TYPE		Insect

Unlike humans, insects don't have lungs. They absorb oxygen through little holes in their sides called spiracles. However, this system isn't always efficient, and if the insect's body is large, it can be difficult to get oxygen to all parts of the body. When the meganeura flourished, there was a lot of oxygen in the atmosphere, but as the number of land animals grew, and the amount of oxygen in the atmosphere fell, these huge insects couldn't get enough oxygen and so became extinct.

PRECAMBRIAN	PALEOZOIC ERA	MESOZOIC ERA	CENOZOIC ERA
	CAMBRIAN PERIOD / ORDOVICIAN PERIOD / SILURIAN PERIOD / DEVONIAN PERIOD / CARBONIFEROUS PERIOD / PERMIAN PERIOD	TRIASSIC PERIOD / JURASSIC PERIOD / CRETACEOUS PERIOD	PALEOGENE PERIOD / NEOGENE PERIOD / QUATERNARY PERIOD

MEGANEURA

Couldn't breathe

Watch your backs! Coming through! The largest insects the world has ever seen!

Where are we going? Ask the wind, my darling. I know we look like dragonflies, but we can hardly move our wings at all. We just let the wind blow us wherever it's going. Whee! Every day's a nice little adventure!

There was a lot of oxygen in our time. Beautiful stuff! Today it's just 20 percent of the air, but back then it was 35 percent. Hit the spot, I tell you! That's why we got so big!

But over time, more and more large land animals appeared. With that lot all breathing, the amount of oxygen in the air fell. And so did we! Couldn't get the oxygen we wanted, so we dropped right out of the sky.

Not very bright

The tusks go in here. ↑

THYLACOSMILUS

Regrets?
Maybe we should have developed a better brain instead of longer teeth.

TIME OF EXTINCTION	Neogene period (late Pliocene epoch)
SIZE	5 feet (1.5 meters) body length
AREA	South America
FOOD	Large mammals
TYPE	Mammal

The thylacosmilus (a marsupial) and the saber-toothed tiger (a placental mammal) are different species, but their appearance and hunting style are very similar. The big difference between them is thought to have been intelligence. Placental mammals have more highly developed brains than marsupials, and the saber-toothed tiger was probably better at thinking of efficient ways of hunting. If they were going after the same prey, the thylacosmilus would probably have lost out.

PRECAMBRIAN | PALEOZOIC ERA (CAMBRIAN PERIOD, ORDOVICIAN PERIOD, SILURIAN PERIOD, DEVONIAN PERIOD, CARBONIFEROUS PERIOD, PERMIAN PERIOD) | MESOZOIC ERA (TRIASSIC PERIOD, JURASSIC PERIOD, CRETACEOUS PERIOD) | CENOZOIC ERA (PALEOGENE PERIOD, NEOGENE PERIOD, QUATERNARY PERIOD)

saber-toothed tiger

Too stupid

Ah! Mr. Saber-Toothed Tiger? I heard you moved into the area recently. Nice to meet you!

Well, I must say we look very similar, don't we? How strange!

What? Imitating you? Certainly not! Mr. S., please, there's no reason to glare at me like that!

But, of course, it's not just a matter of appearance. We hunt the same animals and in the same way. . . . We should cooperate!

Oh dear! Are you ignoring me? Perhaps you've been watching me hunt . . . so that you could take a shortcut and grab my prey. . . .

I'm afraid I'm not very good at thinking things through. I always go off hunting in my usual leisurely way, but when I close in on my prey, I find these days there's nothing there. It's getting awkward.

Would you mind leaving some for me? I'd really appreciate it.

Hey! Croc! What you doing on my territory, scumbag? *I don't look very well?* Don't give me that! I don't like heat. A big fella like me takes time to cool down.

What? *Why don't I move somewhere cooler?* You prawn! I hate the cold even more! Don't you know I can't adjust my body temperature? Anything under 86° Fahrenheit, I can't move at all.

Regrets?
I wish we'd been smaller.

The titanoboa was the world's largest snake—forty-six feet long, three feet diameter, and was estimated to weigh over one ton. That's five times the weight of today's heaviest land snake, the giant anaconda. The titanoboa grew big living beside water after the extinction of the dinosaurs. With no major rivals or predators, it likely hunted other large animals, including crocodiles. However, it is thought to have grown too big to be able to control its body temperature effectively. Active only in a range of 86 to 93° Fahrenheit, it died out when air temperatures got too high.

It was the crocodile that survived in the end.

TIME OF EXTINCTION	Paleogene period (Paleocene epoch)
SIZE	43 feet (13.1 meters) total length
AREA	South America
FOOD	Crocodiles
TYPE	Reptile

PRECAMBRIAN | PALEOZOIC ERA (CAMBRIAN PERIOD, ORDOVICIAN PERIOD, SILURIAN PERIOD, DEVONIAN PERIOD, CARBONIFEROUS PERIOD, PERMIAN PERIOD) | MESOZOIC ERA (TRIASSIC PERIOD, JURASSIC PERIOD, CRETACEOUS PERIOD) | CENOZOIC ERA (**PALEOGENE PERIOD**, NEOGENE PERIOD, QUATERNARY PERIOD)

Look, Crocky, everything's got its upside and its downside. If you're small, you're weak but you're light. If you're big, you're strong but your body ain't flexible.

So if the temperature goes up a bit, that's me finished. Kaput. Extinct!

Couldn't cope with heat or cold

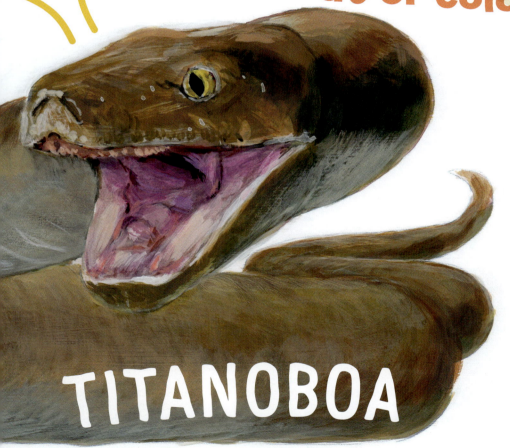

TITANOBOA

Hey, kids! Wanna hear a bit about me? Come over here and take a look at these antlers. Cool, huh? You're gazing at over thirty points there.

Me? What am *I* doing here? Sure. . . . Well, turns out, I got my antlers stuck in the branches of a tree. Can't move an inch.

We started out life in the forest, but we kept getting our magnificent antlers stuck, so we moved to the marshes. But then a lot of humans came to live there too, and there wasn't so much grass for us anymore. And the humans hunted us for our antlers—to use as medicine or to display on their walls. Pretty gross, huh, humans?

By the way, kids, could you just help me slip my antlers out of this tree?

Regrets?
Smaller antlers might have helped. . . .

TIME OF EXTINCTION	1938
SIZE	4 feet (1.2 meters) shoulder height
AREA	Thailand
FOOD	Grass
TYPE	Mammal

Most deer eat soft leaves in forests and woodland, but Schomburgk's deer found forest life difficult because their antlers kept getting stuck in branches. So instead, they lived off the soft grasses in marshland beside Thailand's Chao Phraya River. But with the nearby development of the Thai capital nearby, their habitats were converted into paddy fields, and they were hunted to extinction for their splendid antlers.

SCHOMBURGK'S DEER

Antlers too splendid

The ultimate in male aesthetics

All that rustling!

Can't maneuver!

Regrets?
I wish the sail fin could have been folded down.

TIME OF EXTINCTION	Early Permian period
SIZE	10 feet (3 meters) total length
AREA	America
FOOD	Large animals
TYPE	Synapsid

The dimetrodon looks like a dinosaur, but it was actually a synapsid, a type of animal halfway between an amphibian and a mammal. The dimetrodon flourished as one of the largest meat-eaters of the early Permian period, when temperatures were cold. The sail fin on their backs must have been very useful at that time, allowing them to heat up quickly by increasing their exposure to morning sunlight. But when the atmosphere warmed, the advantage of the sail fin would have been lost, contributing to their gradual extinction.

PRECAMBRIAN	PALEOZOIC ERA						MESOZOIC ERA			CENOZOIC ERA		
	CAMBRIAN PERIOD	ORDOVICIAN PERIOD	SILURIAN PERIOD	DEVONIAN PERIOD	CARBONIFEROUS PERIOD	PERMIAN PERIOD	TRIASSIC PERIOD	JURASSIC PERIOD	CRETACEOUS PERIOD	PALEOGENE PERIOD	NEOGENE PERIOD	QUATERNARY PERIOD

DIMETRODON

Sail fin got in the way

Ouch! Caught again! This thing on my back is such a pain!

It looks good, though, doesn't it? Other animals used to be so jealous!

You see, when we were in our prime, the world was colder. Everyone had to spend a long time warming up in the sunshine each morning before they could move.

With this sail on our backs, we could absorb a lot of sunshine quickly. That meant we could get moving sooner than the others and get as much prey as we wanted. Those were the days!

But then the earth got warmer, and the other animals began to move about more freely. And this sail became more bother than it was worth!

In the end, other animals pinched all our food and nesting places, and we died out.

MAMENCHISAURUS
Neck too long

So near and yet so far

Regrets?
If only our necks had been a little shorter and easier to maneuver...

TIME OF EXTINCTION	Late Jurassic period
SIZE	115 feet (35 meters) total length
AREA	China
FOOD	Leaves
TYPE	Reptile

One of the sauropod group of dinosaurs, all with long necks and tails, the mamenchisaurus had the longest neck of the whole group and is assumed to have eaten leaves over a wide area without walking much. But the bones supporting its long neck became too strong, restricting the neck's movement to thirty degrees in any direction. With this limited flexibility, the mamenchisaurus died out without ever expanding its geographical range.

Sorry! It's a terrible inconvenience. I just seem to have grown bigger and bigger. . . . Well, I'm 115 feet in all, but half of that is just neck!

Exactly! You're absolutely right! Neck maintenance is *the* issue. I've developed bones as light as possible, but, to be honest, things never really seem to go that smoothly.

I can't have my neck suddenly breaking, of course, so I had to have a good strong bone at the base. But that's hindered my movements. Think of my neck held straight out in front of me as an hour hand at nine o'clock—well, I can lift it only as far as about ten o'clock. So I can't eat leaves from tall trees, say, like a giraffe can.

But I'll be okay. I can move my neck horizontally so I can eat leaves around shoulder height without having to stretch up. So please don't worry!

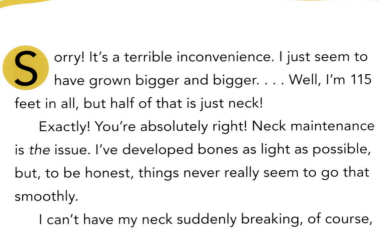

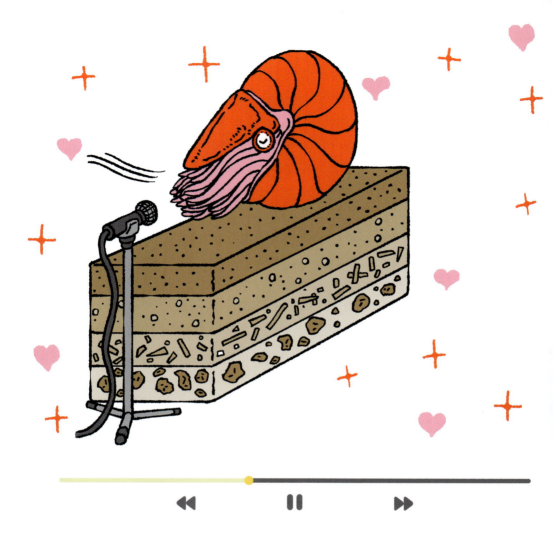

Evolution, save me, I've been feeling so slow

I keep waiting, but I never find my flow...

PART 3

Such a klutz

So Awkward

Breathing, eating, sleeping.
You're doing your best just to live,
so a bit of clumsiness must be okay!
But it may mean you go extinct.

Okay! Here we go again! I *can* fly . . . I *will* fly! Yeah! I think I'm getting the hang of it now.

The real ancestor of birds? No. That's someone else. Yeah, I don't have any descendants at all. That's it.

Hey! You don't have to look so sad! It's okay. Come on! Smile, smile!

Now, I don't have much

Regrets?

If only I'd had more muscle and stronger wings.

← Wing 1

A bird— with teeth!

TIME OF EXTINCTION	Late Jurassic period
SIZE	20 inches (50.8 centimeters) total length
AREA	Germany
FOOD	Insects
TYPE	Bird

The archaeopteryx had wings like a bird but also had clawed forelegs, tailbones, and teeth. It was like an intermediate stage in evolution between a dinosaur and a bird. It couldn't fly, but it could glide, like a flying squirrel. However, it isn't a direct ancestor of modern-day birds. It probably went extinct when flying birds (the ancestors of modern-day birds) appeared, taking its food and living space.

muscle. That's true. But look! I've got wings! Five of them! I'm not good at getting off the ground yet, but I'm good at coming down from high places, right? And my bones are thin, so I'm very light. I think it should be fine. . . .

Great! I'm feeling much better now. Thanks for listening! Okay. Gravity is not a problem! Here goes! Up, up, and— Huh? That's very strange!

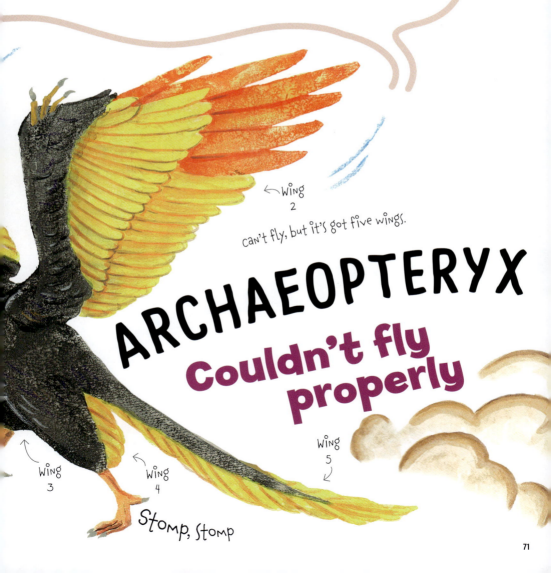

← Wing 2

can't fly, but it's got five wings.

ARCHAEOPTERYX
Couldn't fly properly

Wing 5 ↙

↑ Wing 3

← Wing 4

Stomp, stomp

Shh! Quiet! Oh no! The prey had come so close and now it's run away!

Yeah, I'm the macho type. Long tusks and stuff. And you know what? I used to have a big roar too!

But maybe too much is as bad as too little. You see, I can't run fast at all. All these muscles get in the way! My tail, on the other hand, is too short, so my balance is nothing! Like, I got zero aptitude for agility. I just don't know how to strike that happy medium!

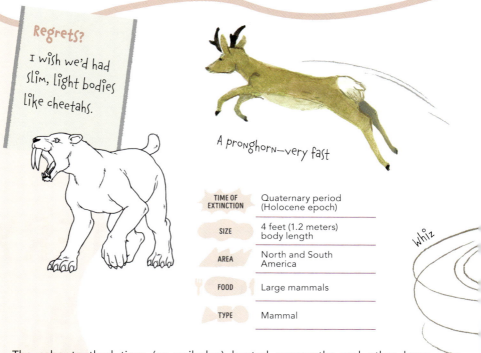

Regrets?
I wish we'd had slim, light bodies like cheetahs.

A pronghorn—very fast

Whiz

TIME OF EXTINCTION	Quaternary period (Holocene epoch)
SIZE	4 feet (1.2 meters) body length
AREA	North and South America
FOOD	Large mammals
TYPE	Mammal

The saber-toothed tiger (or smilodon) hunted mammoths and other large, slow-moving animals, using its front paws to hold its prey and its elongated teeth to rip into flesh. A type of cat, it had short legs and a tail and thick muscles around the neck. This stocky build would have limited its ability to jump and climb trees. It is thought that the saber-toothed tiger went extinct because, when big beasts like mammals died out, they were unable to catch nimbler prey.

PRECAMBRIAN | PALEOZOIC ERA (CAMBRIAN PERIOD, ORDOVICIAN PERIOD, SILURIAN PERIOD, DEVONIAN PERIOD, CARBONIFEROUS PERIOD, PERMIAN PERIOD) | MESOZOIC ERA (TRIASSIC PERIOD, JURASSIC PERIOD, CRETACEOUS PERIOD) | CENOZOIC ERA (PALEOGENE PERIOD, NEOGENE PERIOD, QUATERNARY PERIOD)

I wish I could go back to the days of the mammoth and the megatherium—those big, slow animals were just right for me to hunt. These days the animals are all quick and nimble. It makes life very tough!

That's why I have to creep along like this, keeping downwind so they get no hint that I'm here. Don't go messing things up for me!

Too muscular

I look the part, but I can't move.

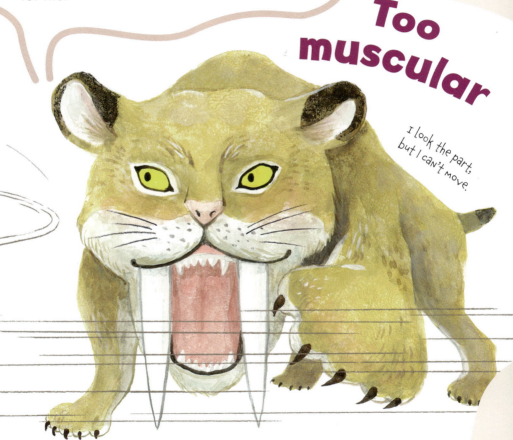

SABER-TOOTHED TIGER (SMILODON)

Looks quick but isn't

Teeth six inches long

Regrets?

If we'd been able to maintain our body temperature like a whale, we could have swum away quickly.

TIME OF EXTINCTION	Neogene period (mid Pliocene epoch)
SIZE	40 feet (12.2 meters) total length
AREA	Tropical and temperate oceans
FOOD	Whales
TYPE	Chondrichthyes (cartilaginous fish)

Three times bigger than the man-eating great white shark (as seen in *Jaws*), and twenty-seven times its weight, the megalodon preyed on whales about thirteen feet long. But things changed when the sea got colder. Whales could move around just as before, but the dip in temperature slowed sharks down. In fact, the whales evolved to swim more quickly, and in the end, the megalodon couldn't cope.

PRECAMBRIAN	PALEOZOIC ERA						MESOZOIC ERA			CENOZOIC ERA		
	CAMBRIAN PERIOD	ORDOVICIAN PERIOD	SILURIAN PERIOD	DEVONIAN PERIOD	CARBONIFEROUS PERIOD	PERMIAN PERIOD	TRIASSIC PERIOD	JURASSIC PERIOD	CRETACEOUS PERIOD	PALEOGENE PERIOD	**NEOGENE PERIOD**	QUATERNARY PERIOD

Whoosh!

MEGALODON
Whales hit back

Scatter! Go! Go! Go! Killer whale! Coming now! Beat a killer? You nuts? Can't be done. They're too strong, too fast. I'm big, but I'm too slow.

Things were good when the sea was warm. I used to eat whales all the time. They weren't so big in them days, and not so fast neither. Hunting them was easy. You could eat your fill, no trouble.

Then the sea got colder. Slowed us right down. But for the whales, it was just the opposite. They evolved. They got quicker! So I couldn't eat them any longer. And in the end, the killer whale appeared—a complete monster—so quick and strong, and it started hunting me! Evolution's a nasty business!

You idiot! This trilobite is as hard as nails! How am I going to eat something like that?

Have you not the slightest notion who I am? Let me enlighten you! I am anomalocaris—the Cambrian king! When all other creatures were less than four inches long, I alone measured over three whole feet!

I have excellent eyes too. I can spin them around in any direction I choose. In the old days, I'd see a nice soft trilobite and I'd snaffle it up straightaway.

But now those trilobites have evolved. They have developed harder shells to protect themselves. They have even gone so far as to grow sharp spines!

My teeth are not very strong, so obviously I CANNOT EAT THEM LIKE THIS!

Somebody! Bring me a fresh-molted ammonite *now*!

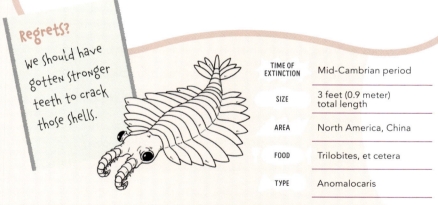

Regrets? We should have gotten stronger teeth to crack those shells.

TIME OF EXTINCTION	Mid-Cambrian period
SIZE	3 feet (0.9 meter) total length
AREA	North America, China
FOOD	Trilobites, et cetera
TYPE	Anomalocaris

The largest sea animal of the Cambrian period, the anomalocaris was the monarch of the deep. Compared to other creatures of the time, it had highly developed eyes and fins. It had no legs and probably used the two thick feelers at the front of its head to catch prey and bring it to its mouth. It is thought that the anomalocaris couldn't eat anything very hard, and that it died out as populations of hard-bodied animals gradually increased.

PRECAMBRIAN | PALEOZOIC ERA (CAMBRIAN PERIOD, ORDOVICIAN PERIOD, SILURIAN PERIOD, DEVONIAN PERIOD, CARBONIFEROUS PERIOD, PERMIAN PERIOD) | MESOZOIC ERA (TRIASSIC PERIOD, JURASSIC PERIOD, CRETACEOUS PERIOD) | CENOZOIC ERA (PALEOGENE PERIOD, NEOGENE PERIOD, QUATERNARY PERIOD)

ANOMALOCARIS

Weak teeth

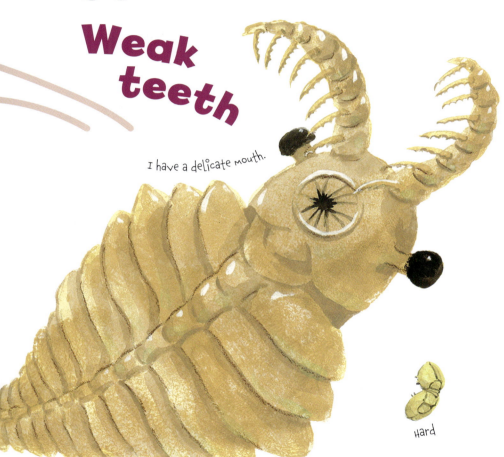

I have a delicate mouth.

Hard

munch, munch, munch, munch, munch, munch, munch

Ten times the appetite of an elephant

Makes a full-grown rhino looks like a child

Regrets?

I wish we could have gotten used to eating grass. Munch munch.

TIME OF EXTINCTION	Paleogene period (late Oligocene epoch)
SIZE	18 feet (5.5 meters) shoulder height
AREA	Eurasian continent
FOOD	Tree leaves and branches
TYPE	Mammal

The largest-ever land mammal, the paraceratherium was a relative of the rhinoceros, though much heavier—at twenty tons, it was twenty times the weight of a black rhino. Unlike rhinos, they had no horns, but males are thought to have used their heads to fight. Their height let them monopolize tree leaves at high levels. It is thought they died out when, as the atmosphere grew drier and there were fewer trees, they couldn't find enough to eat.

PRECAMBRIAN	PALEOZOIC ERA						MESOZOIC ERA			CENOZOIC ERA		
	CAMBRIAN PERIOD	ORDOVICIAN PERIOD	SILURIAN PERIOD	DEVONIAN PERIOD	CARBONIFEROUS PERIOD	PERMIAN PERIOD	TRIASSIC PERIOD	JURASSIC PERIOD	CRETACEOUS PERIOD	**PALEOGENE PERIOD**	NEOGENE PERIOD	QUATERNARY PERIOD

PARACERATHERIUM
Ate too much

Wow! That tastes good! Sooooo good! These leaves! What an aroma! I could go on eating them forever!

Sorry! Got a bit carried away. As you can see, I'm big. Twenty-three feet head to toe. So I have to spend twenty hours a day eating just to stay alive. *Belch!*

By the way, a friend of mine—a real big guy—put one foot in a marsh, and that was that. Fell over and couldn't get up. Just too heavy. Sank without a trace.

So, anyway, we were okay when we lived in the forest, but as the earth gradually got colder and the air drier, the trees began to die off—*burp*—and we were left with nothing but prairie. Eating grass was a heck of a job—all that dipping your head down and lifting it up again—*munch munch*—and there was never enough of the green stuff we needed. So in the end—*Hiccup!* Excuse me—we died of hunger. *Munch.*

DUNKLEOSTEUS

Impenetrable armor

Teeth like a trap of iron

Regrets?

It was our fate to be born at such a time. Nothing could have changed our destiny.

TIME OF EXTINCTION	Late Devonian period
SIZE	33 feet (10 meters) total length
AREA	North America, Africa
FOOD	Fish
TYPE	Placoderm

Dunkleosteus flourished in the Devonian period, until the first trees appeared on the earth. At that time, organisms that break down plant material, like fungi and white ants, had not yet evolved, and so a great deal of this material flowed down rivers into the sea, where the nutrients from the dead plants were absorbed by plankton. As a result, the amount of plankton in the ocean grew enormously, using up a huge amount of the oxygen in the water. As a result, over 80 percent of sea creatures died out, including the dunkleosteus.

PRECAMBRIAN	PALEOZOIC ERA						MESOZOIC ERA			CENOZOIC ERA		
	CAMBRIAN PERIOD	ORDOVICIAN PERIOD	SILURIAN PERIOD	**DEVONIAN PERIOD**	CARBONIFEROUS PERIOD	PERMIAN PERIOD	TRIASSIC PERIOD	JURASSIC PERIOD	CRETACEOUS PERIOD	PALEOGENE PERIOD	NEOGENE PERIOD	QUATERNARY PERIOD

Not enough oxygen

Greatness will pass. The strong will always grow weak. Such is destiny.

I was the monarch of the seas 350 million years ago. My body was protected by plates of bone as hard as armor.

I was huge—thirty-three feet long. My jaws were more powerful even than those of the tyrannosaurus. I had no rival.

Yet I was destroyed by a form of life less than one millimeter in size—phytoplankton*. What mischievous tricks fate can play!

It was a time when large plants had begun to grow on land. When dead material from these plants was washed into the sea, it provided nutrition for phytoplankton.

As the amount of phytoplankton in the ocean grew, the amount of oxygen fell. And the pitiful upshot was that my entire clan suffocated. How the mighty have fallen!

*Phytoplankton: plankton that float in water and, like plants, create energy from sunlight

Blow! Oh, wind! Blow!

Come on! I've been standing here like this for over three hours. It's exhausting, keeping my wings up. And I feel very vulnerable. Not to mention, cold!

Wind! Blow! Oh, wind! *Why* won't you blow? If you don't blow, I can't fly. I weigh over 175 pounds, so I rely on you. And if I can't fly, I can't look for carcasses from up in the sky, and I can't eat. No flight, no food.

Wind! Oh, wind! You've disappeared, haven't you? Must be because the earth has gotten colder. In the old days, when it was hot, there was always a strong wind blowing toward the Andes. . . .

Regrets?
If we'd been lighter, we'd have been able to fly on our own.

TIME OF EXTINCTION	Neogene period (late Miocene epoch)
SIZE	5 feet (1.5 meters) body length
AREA	South America
FOOD	Mammal carcasses
TYPE	Bird

The argentavis was the largest bird ever to have been able to fly, with a wingspan of 23 feet and a weight of 175 pounds. Yet a bird has to be no more than about 35 pounds to fly relying simply on its own strength. So how did the argentavis fly? It seems to have used "updrafts"—air currents rising from warm ground. But when the climate became colder, these updrafts weakened, and the argentavis died out, no longer able to fly.

ARGENTAVIS

Wind stopped blowing

Not a breath of wind!!

Land or water? That is the question.

Descended from whales

Neither one thing nor the other

Regrets?
Sometimes, you have to decide to change where you live... maybe.

TIME OF EXTINCTION	Paleogene period (early Eocene epoch)
SIZE	5 feet (1.5 meters) body length
AREA	Pakistan
FOOD	Fish and small mammals
TYPE	Mammal

You'd never guess from its appearance, but the pakicetus is an ancestor of the whales. Originally, pakicetus moved back and forth between land and sea, with a diet of both fish and other animals. Some pakicetus grew better adapted to life in water, and it was this family branch that eventually evolved into whales. Others remained on land but never developed particular specialization for either land or sea, and in the end died out when competitors came on the scene.

PRECAMBRIAN	PALEOZOIC ERA						MESOZOIC ERA			CENOZOIC ERA		
	CAMBRIAN PERIOD	ORDOVICIAN PERIOD	SILURIAN PERIOD	DEVONIAN PERIOD	CARBONIFEROUS PERIOD	PERMIAN PERIOD	TRIASSIC PERIOD	JURASSIC PERIOD	CRETACEOUS PERIOD	**PALEOGENE PERIOD**	NEOGENE PERIOD	QUATERNARY PERIOD

PAKICETUS

I *really* don't know! Should I stay on land? Or should I go into the sea?

My face is a bit like a wolf's, and I've got hooves like a cow, which make me a good runner.

At the same time, I've got thick ear bones, which means I can hear well underwater, which is good for catching fish.

I should be okay wherever—land or water! But, actually, I'm not a great swimmer, so . . . Mmm, I think maybe I'll stay on land . . . ? Such a dilemma!

Anyway, some of my descendants went to live in the sea, and they evolved into whales apparently! Seems a shame, really—they don't look anything like cute little me! It's a shocker, this evolution business!

The rest of my family—those who didn't become whales—stayed on land. They had a lot of competition and ended up extinct.

So really, I suppose I shouldn't have dithered. I should have gone ahead, taken the plunge, and become a sea creature! Right?

Encounter with the unknown

Regrets?

When prey gets scarce, it's better to be small to stay alive.

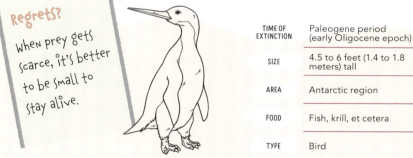

TIME OF EXTINCTION	Paleogene period (early Oligocene epoch)
SIZE	4.5 to 6 feet (1.4 to 1.8 meters) tall
AREA	Antarctic region
FOOD	Fish, krill, et cetera
TYPE	Bird

The end of the Cretaceous period saw the extinction of the plesiosaurs, the long-necked reptiles that had previously dominated the oceans. It was then that the ancestors of today's penguins emerged. As they evolved to adapt to the sea, their wings grew thicker and shorter, and they could no longer fly. Some species became very large. But it seems that when the whales, which evolved at a later stage, came to the Antarctic, these large penguins lost their prey and became extinct.

Whales came to the Antarctic

GIANT PENGUIN

It happened about thirty-three million years ago. The Antarctic was warmer then than it is now, and I had no enemies, so I could eat plenty of fish, and I grew quite big.

One day, I was swimming along as usual when I saw something in the distance that I'd never seen before. I couldn't quite make it out, but it looked like a big black rock. *That's odd*, I thought. Then the rock started coming closer. *Hang on*, I thought. *Something's not quite right*.

Just at that moment, the rock split open. The top went up, and the bottom went down. It swallowed a whole school of fish. Right in front of me.

I don't know how I got home that day. But from then on, it was much more difficult to find enough fish. I discovered later that it was about that time that whales first came to the Antarctic.

Animals everywhere

Regrets?
We should have stayed quietly eating leaves in the woods, even when they got smaller.

Too many rivals

TIME OF EXTINCTION	Quaternary period (late Pleistocene epoch)
SIZE	7 feet (2.1 meters) shoulder height
AREA	Africa, Eurasian continent
FOOD	Grass
TYPE	Mammal

Despite their appearance, sivatherium are actually relatives of the giraffe. Originally, they ate leaves in forests, but because of the changing climate, forests were shrinking rapidly, leaving grassland instead. Forced out onto the grassland, the sivatherium developed thicker teeth so they could eat hard types of grass. But they had a lot of grass-eating rivals, including relatives of horses and cattle, and, eventually, they lost out to the competition and became extinct.

SIVATHERIUM

teeming herds

Eating grass

Humph. There's no point talking about it now. I was beaten. That's all there is to it.

My forebears used to eat leaves in the forest. But the climate changed—it got drier, and the forest shrank. Gradually, they were forced out onto the grassland. And then when I was born, I was a bit different: I could eat hard types of grass.

I had a lot of rivals. It was them or me. I had to compete. No alternative.

Confidence? What's the point of that? You just eat what's in front of you. That's all you have to do to stay alive.

But . . . for a newcomer like me, it wasn't easy. There were tarpan, zebra, water buffalo, and impala. Pro grass eaters, every one of them.

As I watched the grass all being eaten up around me, I sometimes longed to be eating leaves from a tree.

I miss the water so much!

Regrets?
I wish we'd had skin like a crocodile's that could put up with dryness.

Tusks poking through upper jaw—reason unclear

TIME OF EXTINCTION	Late Triassic period
SIZE	20 feet (6.1 meters) total length
AREA	Rivers worldwide
FOOD	Fish
TYPE	Amphibian

With a long flat body and large head, the pond- and river-living mastodonsaurus was one of the world's biggest amphibians. Its head measured four and a half feet, a quarter of its total length. Juveniles lived in the water and breathed through gills, while adults lived on land and breathed through lungs. They didn't like being dry and couldn't be away from water. It seems that in the dry season they'd pack together around small puddles, and in some cases whole groups died together.

MASTODONSAURUS
Dried out

Come on! Just one leg? Just a bite?

What a life! All I can do is crouch here on the bank. Look at my head! It's so heavy I can hardly walk.

And these teeth! Bottom teeth poking up through my top jaw! Ridiculous! No, they are not nasal hairs, you dolt!

There was quite a stir, you know, when I came on the scene. Everyone was talking about this huge new amphibian—me!

But then what? As soon as the crocodiles appeared, I was on the scrap heap.

Think the world of themselves, crocodiles do! Just because they can put up with a bit of dehydration.

Bah! Why did the river I was living on have to go and dry up? If I'd only been able to cope better with conditions like this, I could have survived too . . .

Over here, now! Bring some water! I'm drying out!

ICHTHYOSTEGA

pointlessly bulky build

I just kind of came to see what it was like, but I shouldn't have bothered.

Regrets?

We should at least have waited until there were big insects.

TIME OF EXTINCTION	Late Devonian period
SIZE	3 feet (0.9 meter) total length
AREA	Greenland
FOOD	Fish
TYPE	Amphibian

The ichthyostega is thought to have been the first vertebrate to walk on land. It evolved from a fish with lungs and thick, fleshy fins. But they were big, and their breastbones grew too strong, so they were slow both in water and on land. During the Devonian period, there wasn't enough prey on land, so coming out of the water ended in failure.

PRECAMBRIAN	PALEOZOIC ERA						MESOZOIC ERA			CENOZOIC ERA		
	CAMBRIAN PERIOD	ORDOVICIAN PERIOD	SILURIAN PERIOD	**DEVONIAN PERIOD**	CARBONIFEROUS PERIOD	PERMIAN PERIOD	TRIASSIC PERIOD	JURASSIC PERIOD	CRETACEOUS PERIOD	PALEOGENE PERIOD	NEOGENE PERIOD	QUATERNARY PERIOD

Came up onto land for no real reason

Hey! Take a seat. Here!

I came out of the river some time back, up onto the land. Big mistake! I thought there'd be a lot of food, but no—nothing but little insects. I tell you, it's getting me down!

Hey! Touch my chest. Gently now! Gently!

Feels hard, huh? Those are my ribs. They're really thick. It's difficult to support a body on land—much more difficult than in the sea. So my ribs developed to be nice and strong, almost like they're joined together.

But because of that, I'm not flexible now. I can't bend easily to left and right, so I can't swim well anymore.

On the other hand. I'm no good at walking either. I'm very slow because my body's so heavy. And I'm always hungry—these insects never fill me up!

Agh! Why did I come out of the water? Why, why, why?!

Coming out of my eggs and I was doing just fine
Gotta gotta be proud   Because I won it all

We started out, it was bliss
How did it end up like this?
In the end we just missed
It was only a miss!

PART 4
Out of Luck

My stars weren't aligned...

The animals on Earth today are those that just happened to survive. On the other hand, extinct animals are those that just happened to die out.

Two cute little fingers on each front arm

Regrets?
Maybe we could have hibernated, like bears.

TIME OF EXTINCTION	End of Cretaceous period
SIZE	40 feet (12.2 meters) total length
AREA	North America
FOOD	Medium to large dinosaurs
TYPE	Reptile

A very large carnivorous dinosaur, the tyrannosaurus appeared in the late Cretaceous period. It was thought to have been able to run at eighteen miles per hour and to have had some ability to maintain consistent body temperature like mammals. But maintaining body temperature took a lot of nutrition, so when a meteorite hit Earth sixty-six million years ago, the tyrannosaurus couldn't survive the subsequent food shortage and went extinct, together with the other dinosaurs. Seventy percent of all species on Earth went extinct at that time.

PRECAMBRIAN	PALEOZOIC ERA	MESOZOIC ERA	CENOZOIC ERA
	CAMBRIAN PERIOD / ORDOVICIAN PERIOD / SILURIAN PERIOD / DEVONIAN PERIOD / CARBONIFEROUS PERIOD / PERMIAN PERIOD	TRIASSIC PERIOD / JURASSIC PERIOD / **CRETACEOUS PERIOD**	PALEOGENE PERIOD / NEOGENE PERIOD / QUATERNARY PERIOD

TYRANNOSAURUS

Meteorite strike

Impossible! A meteorite fell from the sky? Unbeloominglievable! Over six miles in diameter! (Laugh.)

When it hit Earth, up came a tidal wave almost a thousand feet high. Whoa! I was terrified! Thought the planet had melted!

But I wasn't going to be beaten by a bit of water. No. The real problem was what came next. The meteorite sent a huge amount of sand up into the sky, and it made this vast cloud all the way around the planet. Because of that, Earth got very cold. Plants didn't grow, and herbivorous dinosaurs that ate them—the herbies—all died. I tried to keep their spirits up: *Come on! Hang in there, guys! Mind you, if you survive, I'll eat you! Ha!*

Anyway, for a while I lived off their carcasses, but something made me feel that wouldn't be a long-term solution!

And sure enough, the carcasses ran out pretty quickly. So there I was—hungry and *extremely* cold—and that was that. Extinction. Thank you and good night!

Agh! The sea's rising! I don't think we can live here anymore!

I'm a bird, but I can't fly. And I'm not a penguin. We look similar and dive in the same way, but actually we're not closely related at all.

I used to live in a warm place, but humans were hunting us, so I kept moving farther and farther north to get away from them. Eventually, I reached this island, near Iceland. There weren't many of us, but we lived here peacefully for a while.

But then an underwater volcano erupted nearby. This caused a big earthquake, and our island sank under the sea.

If only we'd lived a little longer, we might have been as popular as penguins! It's a terrible shame.

Regrets?
I wish we'd started off living somewhere without humans, like the penguins did.

TIME OF EXTINCTION	1844
SIZE	32 inches (81.3 centimeters) total length
AREA	North Atlantic coast
FOOD	Fish
TYPE	Bird

Great auks were birds that dived in the sea for fish. They were slow movers on land and easy for humans to catch, so they gradually were driven farther north. They settled on an island off Iceland, but it sank following the eruption of a nearby submarine volcano. About fifty auks survived on rocks nearby, but these were all hunted down so that museums could obtain specimens.

PRECAMBRIAN	PALEOZOIC ERA	MESOZOIC ERA	CENOZOIC ERA
	CAMBRIAN PERIOD / ORDOVICIAN PERIOD / SILURIAN PERIOD / DEVONIAN PERIOD / CARBONIFEROUS PERIOD / PERMIAN PERIOD	TRIASSIC PERIOD / JURASSIC PERIOD / CRETACEOUS PERIOD	PALEOGENE PERIOD / NEOGENE PERIOD / QUATERNARY PERIOD

GREAT AUK

Island sank

Desperate straits!

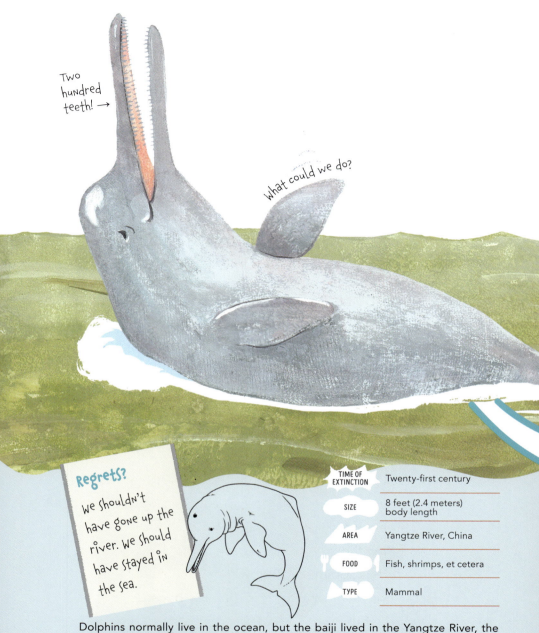

TIME OF EXTINCTION	Twenty-first century
SIZE	8 feet (2.4 meters) body length
AREA	Yangtze River, China
FOOD	Fish, shrimps, et cetera
TYPE	Mammal

Dolphins normally live in the ocean, but the baiji lived in the Yangtze River, the longest river in China. The river water was murky, so their eyes became smaller, and they relied instead on echolocation—judging distance, direction, and size through ultrasound. Evolution of highly mobile necks and large pectoral fins also helped them to avoid obstacles on the riverbed. Their habitat has been seriously damaged by human activity, and it seems highly likely that they are now extinct.

BAIJI (CHINESE RIVER DOLPHIN)

Dirty river

That's enough! It doesn't matter. Forget it! We were stupid to evolve to live on the Yangtze River. I mean, there are four hundred million humans living around there now. With all the houses and factories sending waste into the river, it's bound to be dirty.

And as for the fish the humans catch, well, humans have to live too, right? Though, of course, their fishing meant there wasn't enough prey for us.

And then there were the hydroelectric dams, which prevented us communicating with our fellow dolphins. Plus, all the earth that slid into the river because of logging. But no point fussing about that. We're extinct, after all.

We'd lived in the river for twenty million years. But we should never have settled there in the first place.

Ahh! I reckon I'm done for, boss.
Life was good in the old days—when it was just us on the island. Who could have imagined then that African snails would take it from us? The giant African land snails . . . The way they behaved! After they were brought here by humans as food, they escaped. But they weren't satisfied with just turning wild; they had to go and eat all the humans' crops as well. Not cool!

Regrets?
If we'd been quicker, we could have gotten away.

TIME OF EXTINCTION	Twentieth century
SIZE	0.4 to 0.8 inch (1 to 2 centimeters) shell length
AREA	French Polynesia
FOOD	Plants
TYPE	Gastropod

There are a great number of different types of snail. Because they are slow and only operate within very limited areas, it is easy for different species to develop in different places. The Polynesian tree snails lived in the islands of French Polynesia. Humans living there introduced the giant African land snail, but their population got out of control, so then humans brought in the cannibal snail to eradicate them. But the cannibal snails attacked the Polynesian tree snails, and as a result almost all sixty Polynesian tree snail species became extinct.

PRECAMBRIAN	PALEOZOIC ERA						MESOZOIC ERA			CENOZOIC ERA		
	CAMBRIAN PERIOD	ORDOVICIAN PERIOD	SILURIAN PERIOD	DEVONIAN PERIOD	CARBONIFEROUS PERIOD	PERMIAN PERIOD	TRIASSIC PERIOD	JURASSIC PERIOD	CRETACEOUS PERIOD	PALEOGENE PERIOD	NEOGENE PERIOD	QUATERNARY PERIOD

The humans were angry and brought in the African land snail's natural predators—the cannibal snails. *Serves 'em right*, I thought.

But what happened then? The cannibal snails didn't eat the African land snail punks; they ate us instead. But we hadn't caused no trouble at all! Unbelievable!

Snail warfare

The giant African land snail—the world's largest snail

cannibal snail

About to be eaten

POLYNESIAN TREE SNAIL

Let me tell you of the great magma eruptions of 250 million years ago. A superplume they call it. I call it a nightmare.

The seabed suddenly split open, and out surged a huge mass of magma. There was no comparison with an ordinary eruption of lava. The magma was propelled up through the ocean and over the land as though the very core of the earth had burst free.

Along with the magma came a vast quantity of carbon dioxide, which made the whole planet hot. The amount of oxygen in the atmosphere fell, and animals struggled to breathe. I discovered later that the eruption had caused the extinction of 96 percent of marine species. And, of course, I did not escape.

The same could happen to human civilization. One eruption of magma could wipe it clean away.

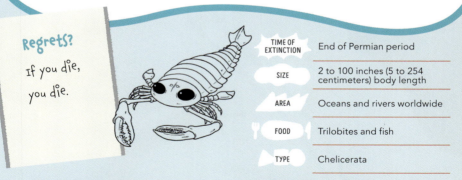

Regrets?
If you die, you die.

TIME OF EXTINCTION	End of Permian period
SIZE	2 to 100 inches (5 to 254 centimeters) body length
AREA	Oceans and rivers worldwide
FOOD	Trilobites and fish
TYPE	Chelicerata

The eurypterids flourished in the seas of the first half of the Paleozoic era, when they had no natural predators. But in the Devonian period, powerful enemies emerged in the form of large carnivorous fish. This signaled the end of the eurypterids' predominance, and from then on, only the smaller eurypterids survived. The eurypterids died out completely because of magma eruptions in the superplume event at the end of the Permian period.

PRECAMBRIAN	PALEOZOIC ERA						MESOZOIC ERA			CENOZOIC ERA		
	CAMBRIAN PERIOD	ORDOVICIAN PERIOD	SILURIAN PERIOD	DEVONIAN PERIOD	CARBONIFEROUS PERIOD	PERMIAN PERIOD	TRIASSIC PERIOD	JURASSIC PERIOD	CRETACEOUS PERIOD	PALEOGENE PERIOD	NEOGENE PERIOD	QUATERNARY PERIOD

SEA SCORPION (EURYPTERID)

Magma misery

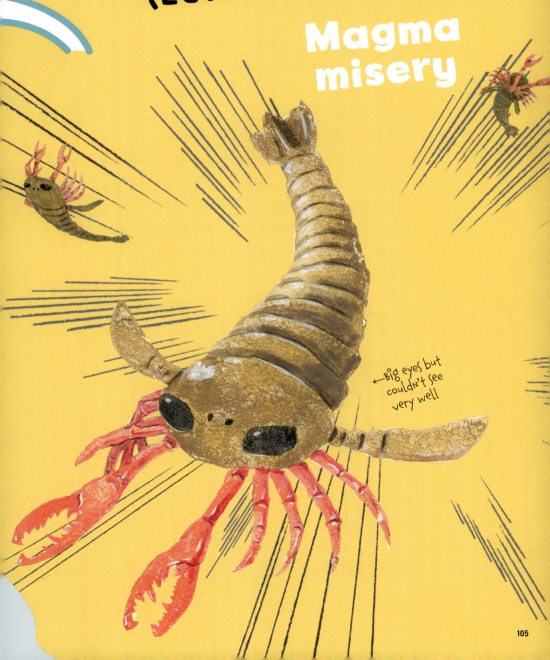

← Big eyes but couldn't see very well

Achoo! I can't stop sneezing! Ugh! What a place! Mount Everest, 29,032 feet high! It's so cold!

It was nowhere near this high up when we were here. We would live off turtles, shellfish, and carcasses we found on the riverbanks and shores that used to be here.

What do you mean *a dull diet*? Who do you think you're talking to? We were the biggest carnivorous mammals ever! Body: thirteen feet long. Head: thirty-three inches long.

We were like bears with crocodile heads!

But 3.4 million years ago, Everest suddenly started getting bigger and bigger. Messed things up for us big-time. Our whole area got cold, and our prey moved away. That was that. Curtains. We were too big, too slow. Got it?

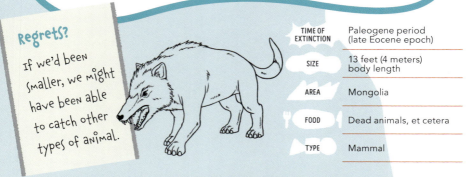

Regrets?
If we'd been smaller, we might have been able to catch other types of animal.

TIME OF EXTINCTION	Paleogene period (late Eocene epoch)
SIZE	13 feet (4 meters) body length
AREA	Mongolia
FOOD	Dead animals, et cetera
TYPE	Mammal

Because of their thirty-three-inch-long skull—the only evidence available—the Andrewsarchus is thought to have been the world's largest carnivorous land mammal. Like a crocodile, it seems to have lived beside warm water. However, when the Indian subcontinent collided with Eurasia, elevating the land and creating Everest and the Himalayas, the Andrewsarchus died out, since its habitat suddenly became too cold and dry.

ANDREWSARCHUS
Everest got higher

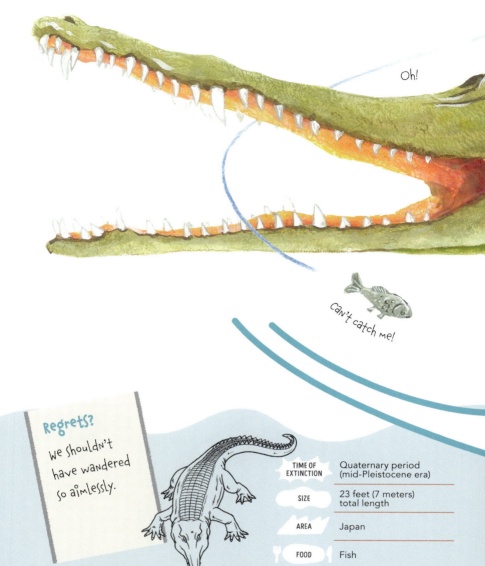

Oh!

Can't catch me!

Regrets?

We shouldn't have wandered so aimlessly.

TIME OF EXTINCTION	Quaternary period (mid-Pleistocene era)
SIZE	23 feet (7 meters) total length
AREA	Japan
FOOD	Fish
TYPE	Reptile

The Toyotamaphimeia was a large crocodile, a fossil of which was found at Machikaneyama in Osaka, Japan. Bigger than the largest species alive today (the saltwater crocodile), it seems to have caught fish with quick, swinging movements of its long, narrow mouth. The Toyotamaphimeia came to Japan when sea levels fell during the Ice Age. As the climate warmed, it ventured deeper inland. When the ice returned, it couldn't get back to the continent, and the cold made its movements sluggish, so it couldn't catch fish and went extinct.

PRECAMBRIAN	PALEOZOIC ERA						MESOZOIC ERA			CENOZOIC ERA		
	CAMBRIAN PERIOD	ORDOVICIAN PERIOD	SILURIAN PERIOD	DEVONIAN PERIOD	CARBONIFEROUS PERIOD	PERMIAN PERIOD	TRIASSIC PERIOD	JURASSIC PERIOD	CRETACEOUS PERIOD	PALEOGENE PERIOD	NEOGENE PERIOD	QUATERNARY PERIOD

TOYOTAMAPHIMEIA

Couldn't escape cold

Oh dear . . . a fish just swam past, right in front of me, but I couldn't move quickly enough. It's the cold that does it. I never realized it would slow me down like this. No.

I think we got the mouth right—it's a good shape for catching fish in the water. I'm pleased with that, I guess.

Maybe we sort of chose the wrong place to live. We didn't really think about it, to be honest. We just headed north. I'd say that was probably a mistake.

We used to be on the Asian continent, and during the Ice Age, we found our way to Japan. Sea levels were very low then, and Japan was linked by land to Russia and Korea, so we could get there walking beside the sea.

But we went too far into Japan. And by the time we realized, it was too late to get back to the continent.

The cold made us slower and slower. We couldn't catch fish to eat, and so in the end, well, we went extinct. Yup.

Oy! What you staring at? Think I'm small, do you? Well, you may just be right! But small ain't weak, blubber boy! This body got things done for more than three hundred million years. Survived three extinction events, when most everything else died out.

What's that face? *But you died out in the fourth one, didn't you?* That what you want to say? Well, blubbie, why don't you try living two hundred million years ago? Whole continents

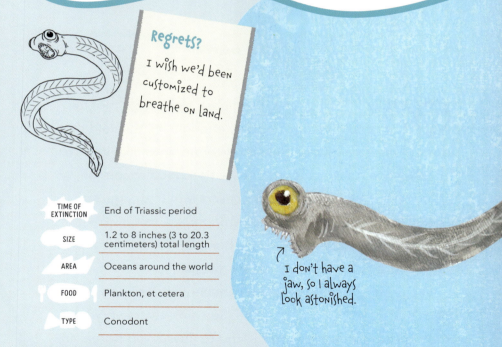

Regrets?
I wish we'd been customized to breathe on land.

TIME OF EXTINCTION	End of Triassic period
SIZE	1.2 to 8 inches (3 to 20.3 centimeters) total length
AREA	Oceans around the world
FOOD	Plankton, et cetera
TYPE	Conodont

I don't have a jaw, so I always look astonished.

"Conodont" was originally the name for tiny tooth fossils, less than one millimeter long, found in layers of rock laid down over three hundred million years, from the Cambrian period to the Triassic period. For over a hundred years after they were first discovered, no one knew what animal they came from. Then, at last, in 1983, a fossil was found that included the remains of the soft part of the animal's body. From that we know that the teeth belonged to a long, narrow-bodied animal. The word "conodont" has now come to be used for the animals themselves.

breaking up, magma spouting everywhere. See how you like it!

Air temperatures rocketed. Water got hot too. And because of all the gases that came up with the magma, it lost all its oxygen!

'Course we went extinct! No way out!

I'll never forgive what them volcanoes done to us. Couldn't breathe!

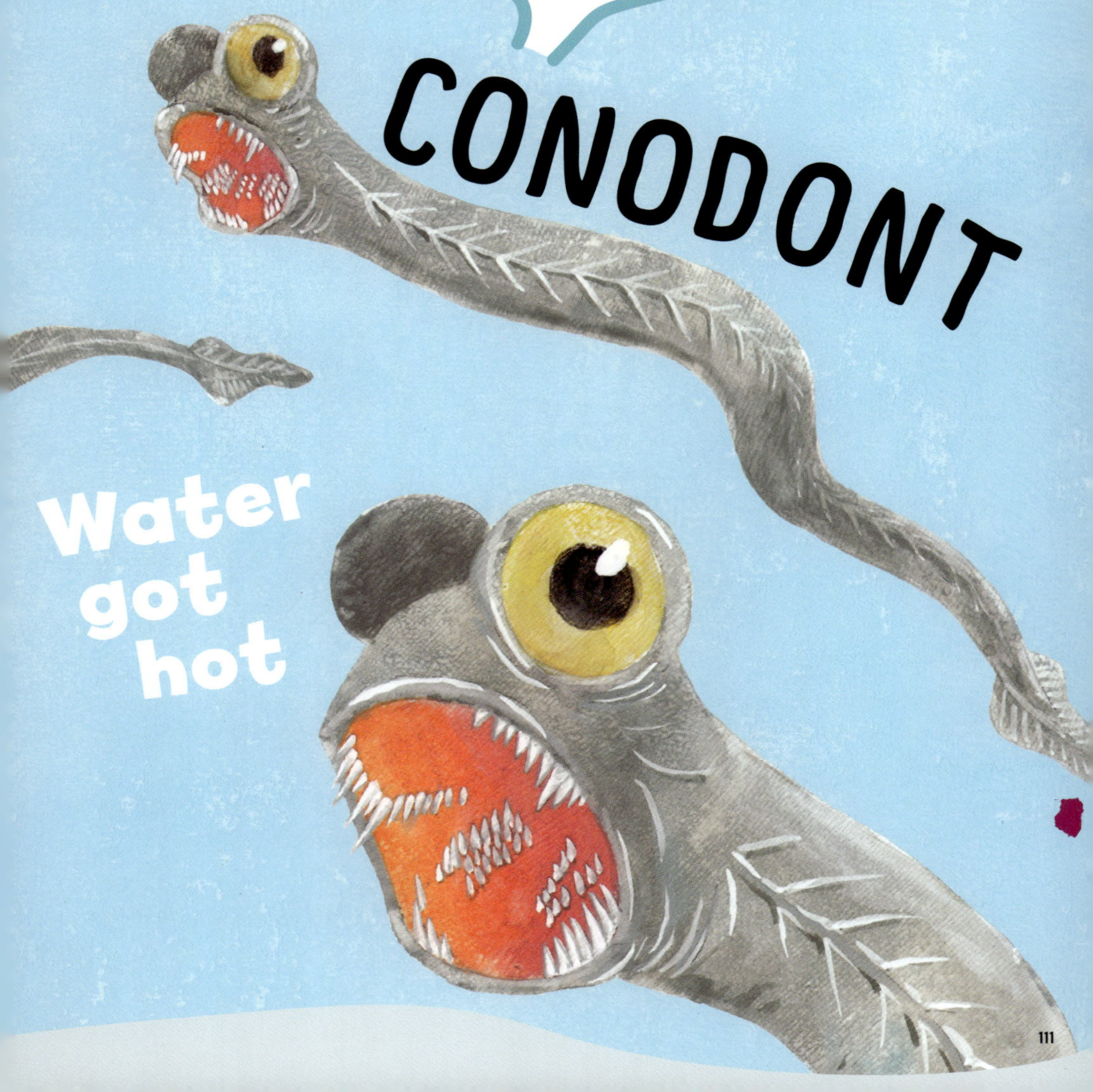
CONODONT
Water got hot

Look at all that snow! The ground's completely white!

We were good in the cold, us mammoths. We had long hairy fur all over to keep the warmth in. We even had a flap of skin to cover our buttholes!

But the earth gradually got warmer, and all the ice around the world started to melt.

Because of that, the atmosphere became more humid and big clouds formed. And in Siberia, where we lived, huge amounts of snow began to fall.

We didn't mind the snow being cold. The problem was the grass. Grass is what we ate, and with snow on the ground for almost half the year, it couldn't grow! We were big animals, and we couldn't get by with just the odd tuft here and there.

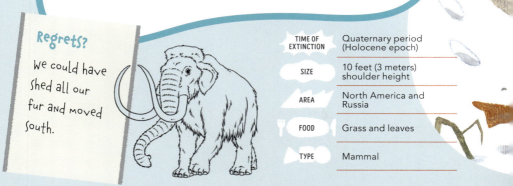

Regrets?
We could have shed all our fur and moved south.

TIME OF EXTINCTION	Quaternary period (Holocene epoch)
SIZE	10 feet (3 meters) shoulder height
AREA	North America and Russia
FOOD	Grass and leaves
TYPE	Mammal

The woolly mammoth's long hair makes it look very large, but it was actually about the same size as the Asian elephant. It lived in cold regions around the Arctic, eating plants that were tolerant of low temperatures. This was possible during the Ice Age because the atmosphere was dry and there wasn't much snow. When the Ice Age ended, however, the rise in temperatures brought increased moisture in the atmosphere, which in cold areas led to heavy snowfall. This meant that the plants the mammoth used to eat could no longer grow so easily, which seems to have led to its extinction.

PRECAMBRIAN	PALEOZOIC ERA	MESOZOIC ERA	CENOZOIC ERA
	CAMBRIAN PERIOD / ORDOVICIAN PERIOD / SILURIAN PERIOD / DEVONIAN PERIOD / CARBONIFEROUS PERIOD / PERMIAN PERIOD	TRIASSIC PERIOD / JURASSIC PERIOD / CRETACEOUS PERIOD	PALEOGENE PERIOD / NEOGENE PERIOD / **QUATERNARY PERIOD**

WOOLLY MAMMOTH

I'm a type of elephant.

Snowfall

This is the end.

Regrets?

maybe we should have just upped and gone to another island.

TIME OF EXTINCTION	1885
SIZE	20 inches (50.8 centimeters) total length
AREA	Cuba
FOOD	Fruits of trees
TYPE	Bird

Macaws lay eggs in holes in thick tree trunks, so they can't live if there are no forests with big trees. But humans had gradually cleared Cuba's forests to make fields. The macaws' habitat had shrunk so much that the only place they had left to live was the coastal mangrove forest. But a series of major hurricanes destroyed the mangrove forest, and the macaws became extinct.

PRECAMBRIAN	PALEOZOIC ERA	MESOZOIC ERA	CENOZOIC ERA
	CAMBRIAN PERIOD / ORDOVICIAN PERIOD / SILURIAN PERIOD / DEVONIAN PERIOD / CARBONIFEROUS PERIOD / PERMIAN PERIOD	TRIASSIC PERIOD / JURASSIC PERIOD / CRETACEOUS PERIOD	PALEOGENE PERIOD / NEOGENE PERIOD / **QUATERNARY PERIOD**

Blown away by a hurricane
CUBAN RED MACAW

Ah! Did you hear that? It was the wind! I am broadcasting live from the Zapata Swamp in Cuba. A major hurricane hit the island about one hour ago.

The wind is ferocious! These trees beside me are mangrove trees. Just look how many have been blown over! Our nests are in these trees. Cuban red macaws used to live all over the island, but then humans started cutting down the forests to make fields. So we all evacuated to this small strip of mangrove forest on the coast.

Look! There goes another mangrove tree! We've had four hurricanes now, and the forest has been almost completely destroyed.

With that, this is me signing off from the Zapata Swamp.

I am a laughing owl. As my name suggests, my laugh-like cry is my identity.

We lived in New Zealand. The forests there were full of our laughter. Then humans arrived.

The humans released rabbits so that they could hunt them. The rabbits bred more quickly than the humans expected and ate the humans' crops. We laughed at the humans' stupidity.

But the humans didn't take the destruction of their crops

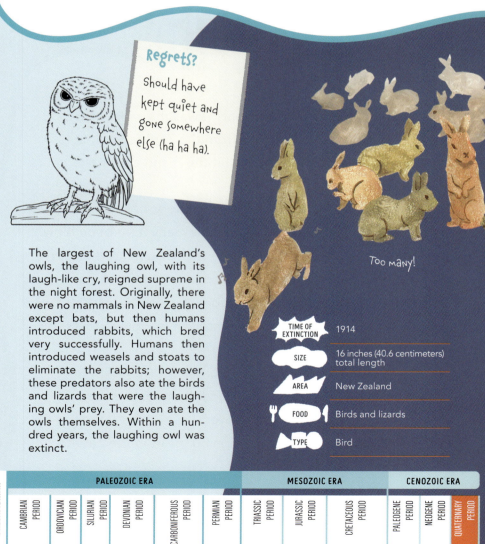

Regrets?
Should have kept quiet and gone somewhere else (ha ha ha).

Too many!

The largest of New Zealand's owls, the laughing owl, with its laugh-like cry, reigned supreme in the night forest. Originally, there were no mammals in New Zealand except bats, but then humans introduced rabbits, which bred very successfully. Humans then introduced weasels and stoats to eliminate the rabbits; however, these predators also ate the birds and lizards that were the laughing owls' prey. They even ate the owls themselves. Within a hundred years, the laughing owl was extinct.

TIME OF EXTINCTION	1914
SIZE	16 inches (40.6 centimeters) total length
AREA	New Zealand
FOOD	Birds and lizards
TYPE	Bird

lying down. They introduced weasels, the rabbits' natural predator.

The weasels ate the rabbits. But they also ate us. Perhaps our laughter made us too easy for them to find.

But had we stopped laughing we would have lost our identity. So we resolved to carry on laughing, and we became extinct.

I was once the monarch of the night.

Laughed too much

LAUGHING OWL

FIGHT!

TRILOBITE SQUADRON
Episode 1: Arrival of the Trilobite Squadron

A: I'm Terataspis! Trilobite hero. Big body and iron defense!

B: I'm Eoharpes! Expert at straining water for food!

C: I'm Kowalewskii! Ninja assassin. I keep watch from the sand with my periscope eyes!

D: I'm Cyrtometopus! Avenger. Attackers are defeated by my spines!

A: We have evolved in multifarious ways and have survived two mass extinctions! We *are* the Trilobite Squadron! *(That went well!)*

B: Captain!

A: Yes?

C: The fish! They're after us!

A: I see. . . . This is the end!

B, C & D: Huh?

A: We cannot beat the fish. We have no future. See you in the next world!

B, C & D: But, Captain!!!

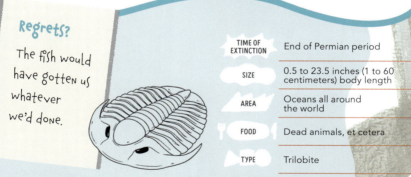

Regrets?
The fish would have gotten us whatever we'd done.

TIME OF EXTINCTION	End of Permian period
SIZE	0.5 to 23.5 inches (1 to 60 centimeters) body length
AREA	Oceans all around the world
FOOD	Dead animals, et cetera
TYPE	Trilobite

Trilobites appeared in the Cambrian period. From the very earliest stages, they had eyes and hard bodies, which made them very successful. But in the Devonian period, fish evolved and feasted on trilobites in spite of their hard bodies. As a consequence, the number of trilobite species shrank dramatically in the Carboniferous period. The few that remained died out in the extinction event at the end of the Permian period.

TRILOBITE

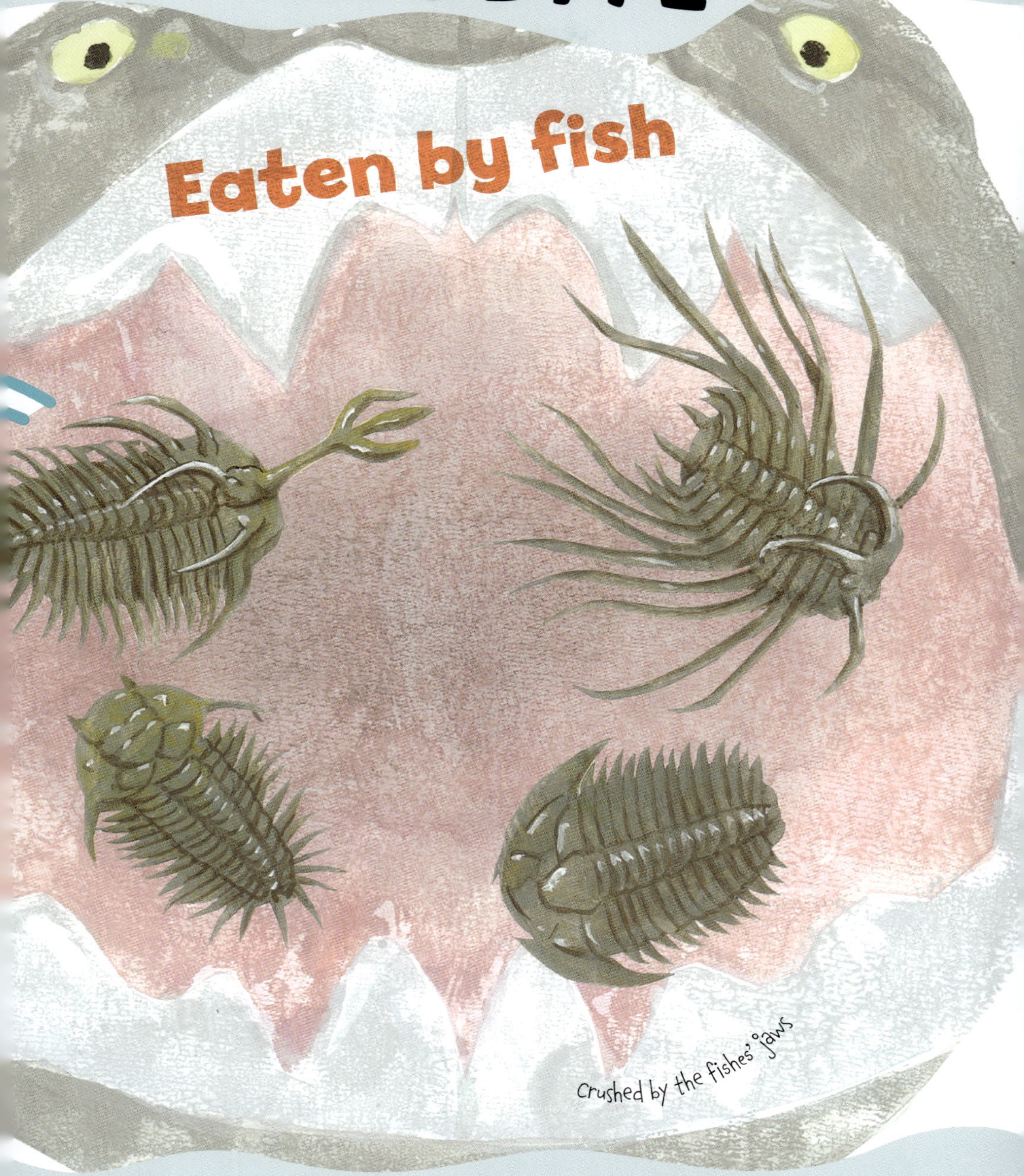
Eaten by fish
Crushed by the fishes' jaws

I wish I could go back in time—to those carefree grass-eating days!

Look at these two horns! Pretty big, huh? But you know what? They're hollow. Empty. We just needed our horns to be big. Didn't care about what was inside.

It was all to impress the women. Every day we'd be waving our horns about, fighting the other guys. We all believed that was what we should do.

But no. While we were spending our time fighting, the climate was changing—it was getting drier. The waterfront areas were gradually shrinking, and the desert was growing. Before we realized it, the desert was all around us.

There's no grass to eat now. My stomach is empty. And a hollow feeling fills my heart. Just like my hollow horns.

Why do we only realize what's important when it's no longer there?

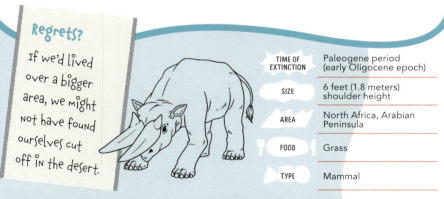

Regrets?
If we'd lived over a bigger area, we might not have found ourselves cut off in the desert.

TIME OF EXTINCTION	Paleogene period (early Oligocene epoch)
SIZE	6 feet (1.8 meters) shoulder height
AREA	North Africa, Arabian Peninsula
FOOD	Grass
TYPE	Mammal

The arsinoitherium lived in swamps and mangrove forests in the region of present-day Egypt. But as the climate changed, the atmosphere grew drier and the area gradually turned into desert. Meanwhile, the Red Sea developed between Africa and the Arabian Peninsula, splitting the arsinoitherium's area of habitation. Stranded in the desert, the animals weren't able to eat enough grass to support their large bodies, and so they died out.

Stranded in the desert
ARSINOITHERIUM

These horns are surprisingly light.

GUAM FLYING FOX: 😨 Oh no! Is this the end? Wiped out by humans?

GUAM FLYING FOX: 😡 We were living in peace on this small island, eating fruit. Seventy years ago, you suddenly came and turned the island into a tourist destination!

GUAM FLYING FOX: 🥺 A lot of humans came, decided we were a local delicacy, and ate us. We will never forget our hatred of you, even when we are dead!

GUAM FLYING FOX: ☠️

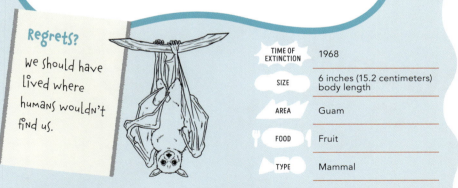

Regrets?
We should have lived where humans wouldn't find us.

TIME OF EXTINCTION	1968
SIZE	6 inches (15.2 centimeters) body length
AREA	Guam
FOOD	Fruit
TYPE	Mammal

Flying foxes are quite popular as food in the tropics, as they are tasty and large enough for a meal. In Guam, the local Chamorro people had always eaten flying fox. But Guam is a very small place, and there were only a few thousand flying foxes living there. When people started trying to catch them to serve to tourists, the flying foxes died out within just twenty years.

Eaten out of curiosity

GUAM FLYING FOX

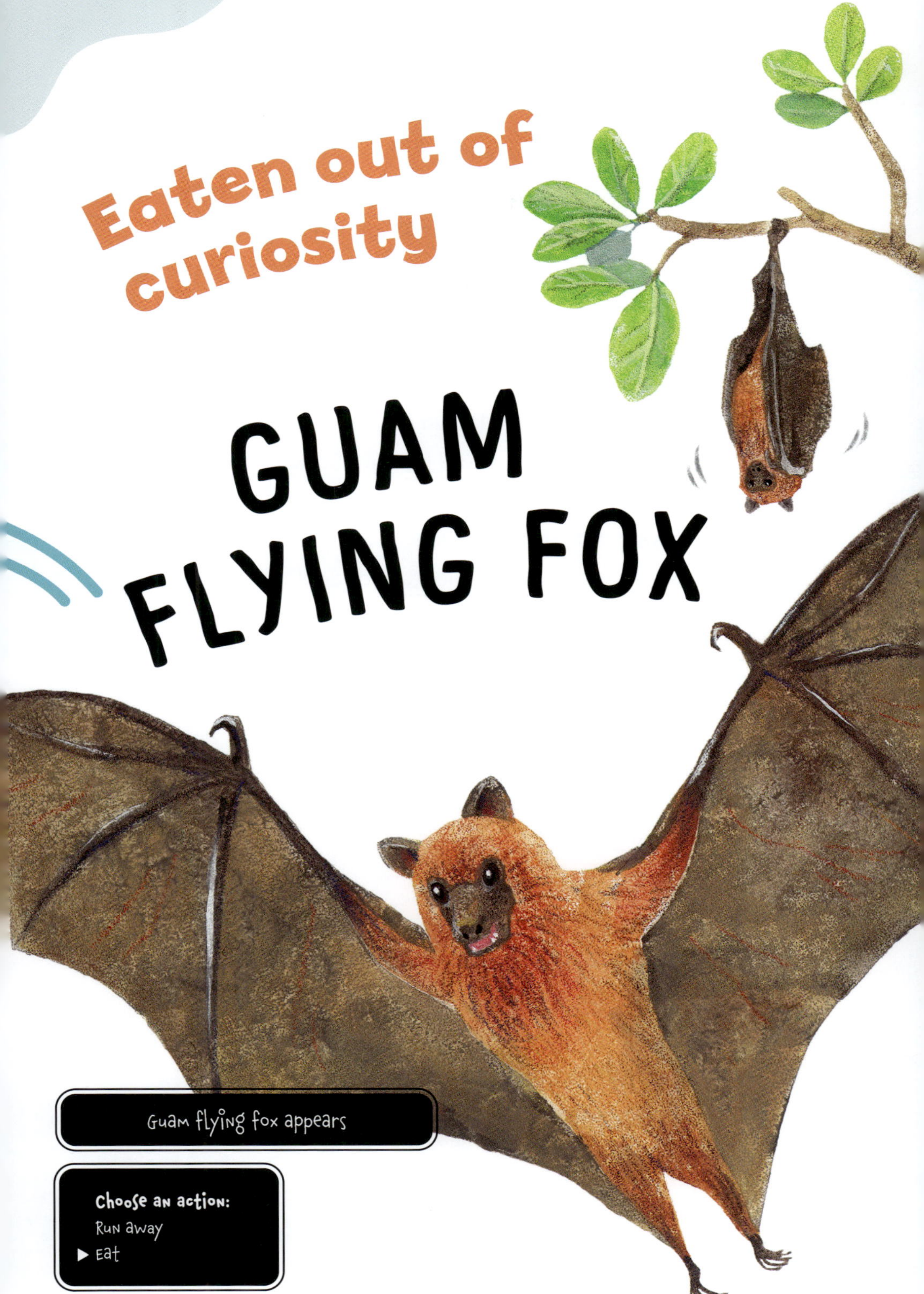

Guam flying fox appears

Choose an action:
Run away
▶ Eat

All the cool kids know me! I'm an idol of the vegetarian dinosaur world!

They like these jagged, leaf-shaped plates on my back, and my thick, spiky tail. And though I'm a vegetarian, I can fight any carnivorous dinosaur and send it packing. That's the kind of thing that steals hearts. I know!

But underneath it all, I'm just an ordinary animal. Even idols have secrets. Don't be shocked! I may be big, but I have a very weak bite. I have no more strength in my jaws than a seventy-year-old human. So when plants started producing flowers, I didn't know what to do. They're so pretty, but their leaves are too tough to chew! All I can eat are very soft plants like ferns.

But flowering plants were very successful very quickly, and as they blossomed, my life withered away.

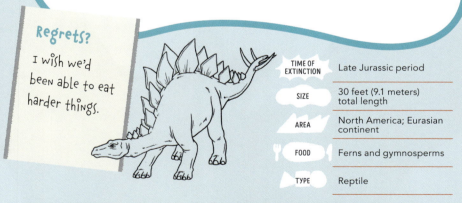

Regrets?

I wish we'd been able to eat harder things.

TIME OF EXTINCTION	Late Jurassic period
SIZE	30 feet (9.1 meters) total length
AREA	North America; Eurasian continent
FOOD	Ferns and gymnosperms
TYPE	Reptile

The stegosaurus was huge but had a very weak bite. One reason was that its head was very small, but another was presumably that it had only ever eaten soft plants. At the end of the Jurassic period, angiosperms (flower-bearing plants) began to appear, and they spread rapidly. This was when the stegosaurus died out—so perhaps the new plants were too tough for their mouths to deal with.

PRECAMBRIAN	PALEOZOIC ERA						MESOZOIC ERA			CENOZOIC ERA		
	CAMBRIAN PERIOD	ORDOVICIAN PERIOD	SILURIAN PERIOD	DEVONIAN PERIOD	CARBONIFEROUS PERIOD	PERMIAN PERIOD	TRIASSIC PERIOD	**JURASSIC PERIOD**	CRETACEOUS PERIOD	PALEOGENE PERIOD	NEOGENE PERIOD	QUATERNARY PERIOD

STEGOSAURUS

This tail could wipe out even a carnivorous dinosaur.

Blooming flowers

A field of flowers—the smell of death...

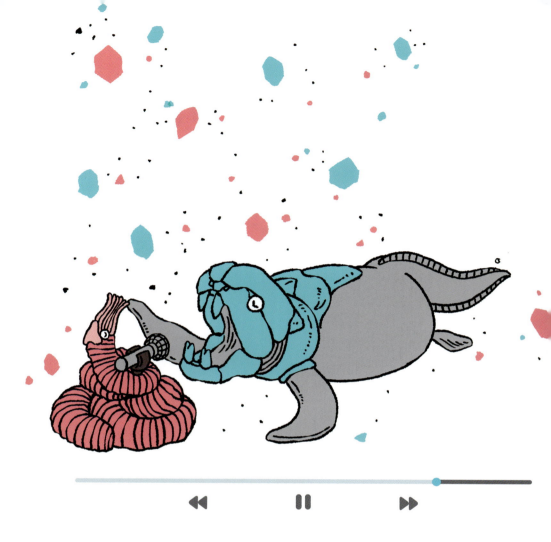

At first I was at risk, and I could have died

Kept thinking I would never live, but then I survived...

PART 5
Made It Out Alive

Sometimes when extinction seems to be on the cards, the animal survives.

It's no great secret, but, um . . . I have a rather unusual body.

Well, for one thing . . . my pee, my poo, and my eggs all come out of the same hole. And also, I'm no good at adjusting my body temperature. I'm a mammal—just like a human—but in some ways I guess maybe I'm more like a reptile or something. I live in the water as well.

Oh dear! It all makes me sound like a crocodile!

Um, anything else . . . ? Well, maybe the way I keep my eyes tightly shut when I'm swimming? I'm sure that's a lot cuter than a crocodile!

Yeah, it's not all bad. Because I live in the water, I don't have to compete much for nests and food with other animals. Out of the water, you get a lot of rivals—most animals we were related to have gone extinct. So I'm glad we ended up in the water!

I mean, we've managed to survive with this strange body for tens of millions of years, so I guess we're pretty lucky!

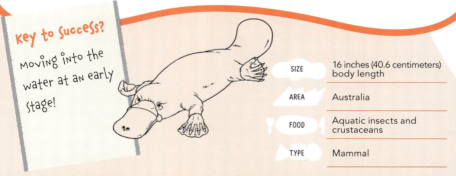

Key to success?
Moving into the water at an early stage!

SIZE	16 inches (40.6 centimeters) body length
AREA	Australia
FOOD	Aquatic insects and crustaceans
TYPE	Mammal

The duck-billed platypus is one of a primitive group of mammals called monotremes. Most monotremes went extinct, after their food sources and nesting sites were taken over by marsupials such as kangaroos. The duck-billed platypus probably survived because it evolved to live in water. Its marsupial rivals hardly ever ventured into the water, since their babies would have died when water got into their pouches.

DUCK-BILLED PLATYPUS

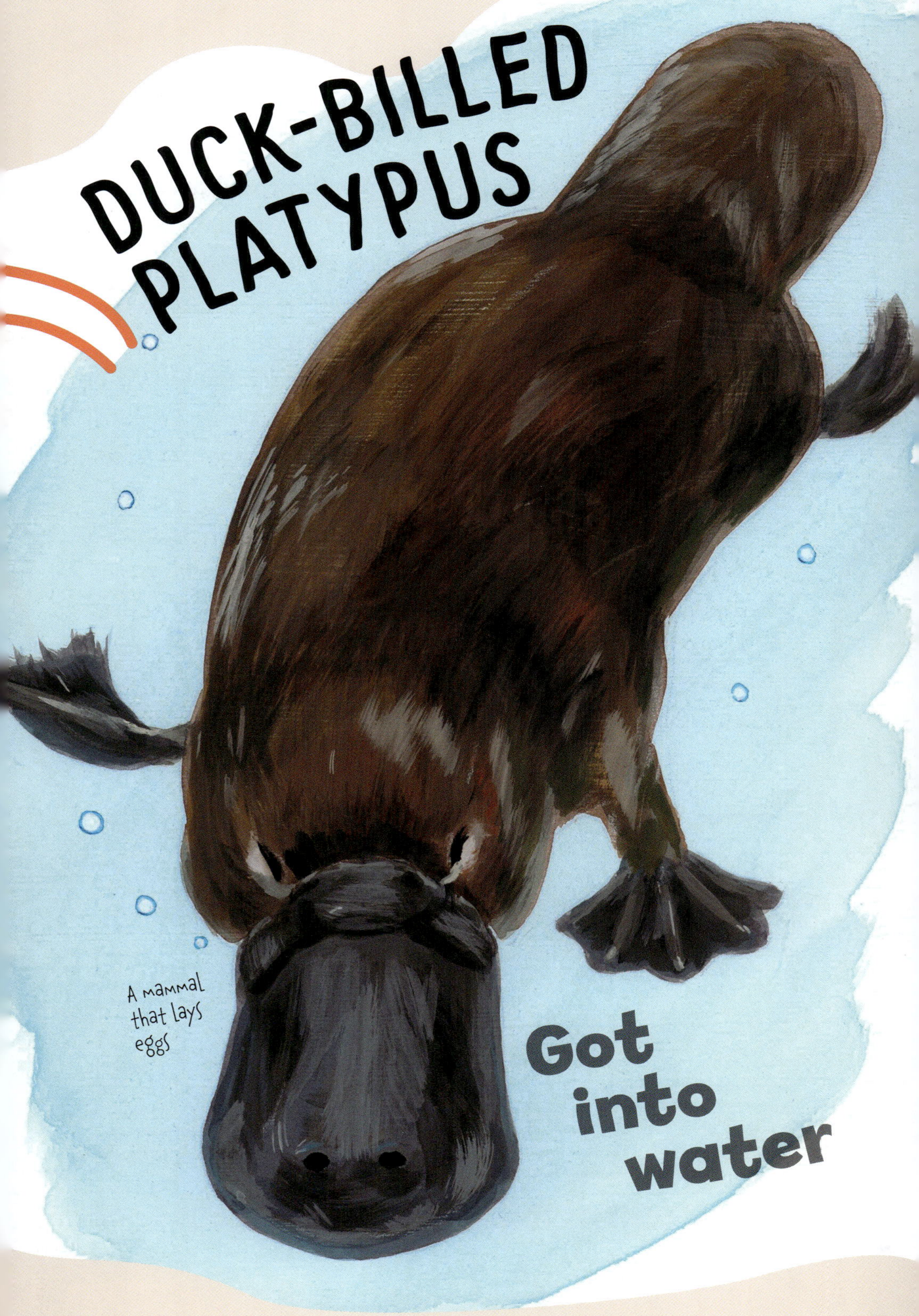
A mammal that lays eggs
Got into water

A: It's no use! I can't run another step.
B: Don't say that! If we stay here, we'll die. Get up!
A: I can't! Look how high the sun is already! Go on without me!
B: I can't leave you here!
A: Why ever did we come to Japan?
B: It was the Ice Age! Even Japan was cold then! We're here now. We just have to face it.
A: I never dreamed it would get so hot after the Ice Age! What are the others doing?
B: They all went back to Russia long ago. We're the only ones here now!
A: Ahh! No, it's too much!
B: Listen to me! We can't live in this heat. There's only one way out. Up! Up the mountain to the snow! Go! Go! Go!
A: I never knew you were so energetic.
B: Hey! I'm a hot-blooded, hotheaded guy. Don't get burned, chick!
A: No worries on that score, at least.

Key to success? When we got stuck in Japan, we moved up the mountains to where it was cold.

SIZE	15 inches (38.1 centimeters) total length
AREA	Honshu, Japan
FOOD	Shoots and seeds
TYPE	Bird

The ptarmigan is normally found in countries with cold climates, such as in Canada or Russia. The reason it is also found in Japan, a much warmer country, is that some moved there during the Ice Age when the whole earth was cold. When the Ice Age ended, some went back north, some died in the heat, but others went up into high mountains, over sixty-five hundred feet in altitude, where they survive today as a subspecies: the Japanese ptarmigan.

PTARMIGAN
Went to the mountains

Road to Survival

What do I do on a day off? Well, to be honest, I like to stay home—never go out of the forest!

I stay home on work days too. I'm just walking around the forest looking for grass, berries, leaves, roots, stuff like that. I really never leave the forest at all.

Why? Well . . . all of us hippos have very sensitive skin. If we're out in the sun for long, we get badly burned. Hippos who live in the savanna spend daytime quietly lolling about in the water. Where I live in the forest, though, it's very humid. The mist acts as a kind of natural moisturizer!

So, as long as I stay in the forest, I can live without a river.

Also, I'm slim, so I can walk faster than other hippos. Don't tell anyone I said that though!

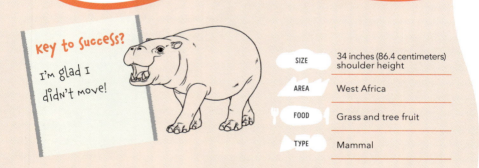

Key to success?
I'm glad I didn't move!

SIZE	34 inches (86.4 centimeters) shoulder height
AREA	West Africa
FOOD	Grass and tree fruit
TYPE	Mammal

When the earth's temperature fell and the atmosphere became drier, the world's total forest area shrank rapidly, and in Africa, areas of savanna and desert grew. This led a lot of leaf-eating mammals to move out of the forest. Pygmy hippopotamuses, however, stayed where they were. As a result, although their habitat is now limited to parts of western Africa, they have survived and still look exactly as their ancestors did.

Stayed in the woods

PYGMY HIPPOPOTAMUS

No point talking about me. It'd be much more interesting to hear about everyone else.

No, really, I'm dull as ditch water. I don't eat a lot. I grow very slowly. Not much in the way of weapons.

If I had to say something positive about myself, I suppose it'd be that I can handle the cold and, well, that I can live to over a hundred years. I wish I could say something more exciting than that, but . . .

Key to success?

The safest way is to keep quiet and not draw attention to yourself.

Eight years old

Hey! It's a tuatara!

SIZE	24 inches (61 centimeters) total length
AREA	New Zealand
FOOD	Insects and lizards
TYPE	Reptile

It looks like a lizard, but the tuatara is classified as belonging to its own, quite distinct group of reptiles. Tuataras used to live in many parts of New Zealand, but now they are only found on thirty islands, where a critical factor in their survival has been the absence of humans, livestock, et cetera. They can live over a hundred years and don't eat much, so without enemies, they've been able to keep going quietly for a very long time.

(INCLUDES ALL SPECIES OF THE TUATARA GROUP)

PRECAMBRIAN	PALEOZOIC ERA						MESOZOIC ERA			CENOZOIC ERA		
	CAMBRIAN PERIOD	ORDOVICIAN PERIOD	SILURIAN PERIOD	DEVONIAN PERIOD	CARBONIFEROUS PERIOD	PERMIAN PERIOD	TRIASSIC PERIOD	JURASSIC PERIOD	CRETACEOUS PERIOD	PALEOGENE PERIOD	NEOGENE PERIOD	QUATERNARY PERIOD

In fact, I only survived by chance, really. I lived on a small island where no humans ever came, so they didn't bring dogs and rats and so on. I was just lucky.

Rats would have finished us off. We only lay eggs once every four years. If they got eaten, we'd be extinct in no time.

Low profile— long life

108 years old

Ah... it's a tuatara!

ONE HUNDRED YEARS LATER

TUATARA

I feel *so* sluggish! Swimming is such a pain. It's just not my thing. I mean, I can only move at two inches a second. It'd take me an hour to get around a school playground!

And I can't be bothered with eating. When was the last time I had some food? Five days ago . . . ?

Well, that'll keep me going for another two days. A bit of old fish once a week is enough to keep me alive.

I can't be bothered with conflict either. A long time ago, I used to live in shallow parts of the sea, but I got fed up with all the competition. I'm so slow, they took everything! ME ME ME! That was their attitude. I don't like that type at all. So I slipped away and started living a quiet life deeper in the sea.

Then, suddenly, a meteor hit Earth, and the dinosaurs and so on were all killed off. Apparently, almost everything in the shallows was destroyed.

But it's none of my business. It didn't affect me. I don't really care what happened.

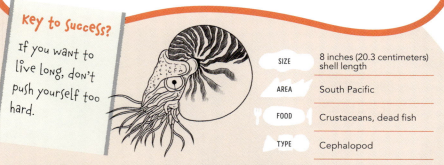

Key to success?
If you want to live long, don't push yourself too hard.

SIZE	8 inches (20.3 centimeters) shell length
AREA	South Pacific
FOOD	Crustaceans, dead fish
TYPE	Cephalopod

The nautilus is a survivor of a group that appeared in the Cambrian period, over five hundred million years ago. Originally, they lived in shallow seas, but they weren't as quick as other cephalopods (like ammonite and squid), so they were gradually edged out to the deeper ocean, where there was less food. But they were lucky this happened. The shallow seas were badly damaged in the extinction event at the end of the Cretaceous period, while the deeper ocean was not much affected.

(INCLUDES ALL NAUTILUS-TYPE SPECIES)

PRECAMBRIAN	PALEOZOIC ERA						MESOZOIC ERA			CENOZOIC ERA		
	CAMBRIAN PERIOD	ORDOVICIAN PERIOD	SILURIAN PERIOD	DEVONIAN PERIOD	CARBONIFEROUS PERIOD	PERMIAN PERIOD	TRIASSIC PERIOD	JURASSIC PERIOD	CRETACEOUS PERIOD	PALEOGENE PERIOD	NEOGENE PERIOD	QUATERNARY PERIOD

Fish are so energetic!

Couldn't be bothered
NAUTILUS

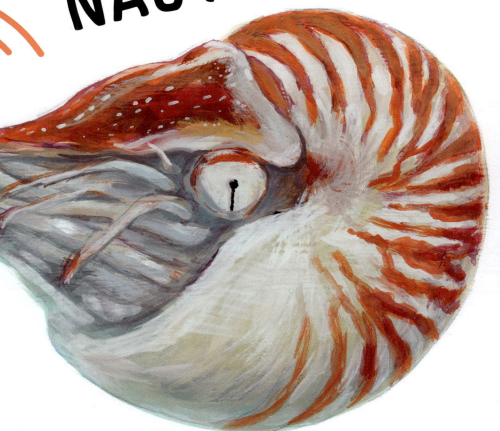
Gave up competing in shallow water

THE ADVENTURE OF THE TREE LOBSTER

Chapter 1: A Desperate Escape

That night, I set out across the ocean, clinging to a piece of rotten driftwood. Destination unknown. It was a desperate escape!

It was tough to tear myself away from Lord Howe Island. I had lived there so long. But humans had come, and staying there meant danger. They called us land crayfish and used us as fishing bait. We could just about have survived that. The real problem was black rats. They'd arrived with the humans and they ate huge numbers of us. We were on the verge of extinction. There was nothing else for it. I knew I had to go.

When I woke up the next day, I found myself at the foot of a huge pyramid of rock. I'd been swept onto an uninhabited island. I saw some vegetation—not much, but some. I decided there and then: *I'm going to start afresh right here—my new home.*

Chapter 2: The Arrival of the Rock Climbers . . .

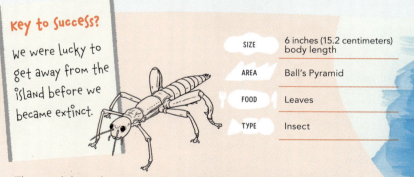

Key to Success?
We were lucky to get away from the island before we became extinct.

SIZE	6 inches (15.2 centimeters) body length
AREA	Ball's Pyramid
FOOD	Leaves
TYPE	Insect

The tree lobster became extinct in 1920 in its original home, Australia's Lord Howe Island, after the arrival of black rats. But in the 1960s, a dead tree lobster was found by rock climbers ten miles away on Ball's Pyramid, a 1,843-foot-high rock island where only short vegetation grows. More recently, a survey on Ball's Pyramid confirmed the existence of a living population of tree lobsters there.

PRECAMBRIAN | PALEOZOIC ERA (CAMBRIAN PERIOD, ORDOVICIAN PERIOD, SILURIAN PERIOD, DEVONIAN PERIOD, CARBONIFEROUS PERIOD, PERMIAN PERIOD) | MESOZOIC ERA (TRIASSIC PERIOD, JURASSIC PERIOD, CRETACEOUS PERIOD) | CENOZOIC ERA (PALEOGENE PERIOD, NEOGENE PERIOD, QUATERNARY PERIOD)

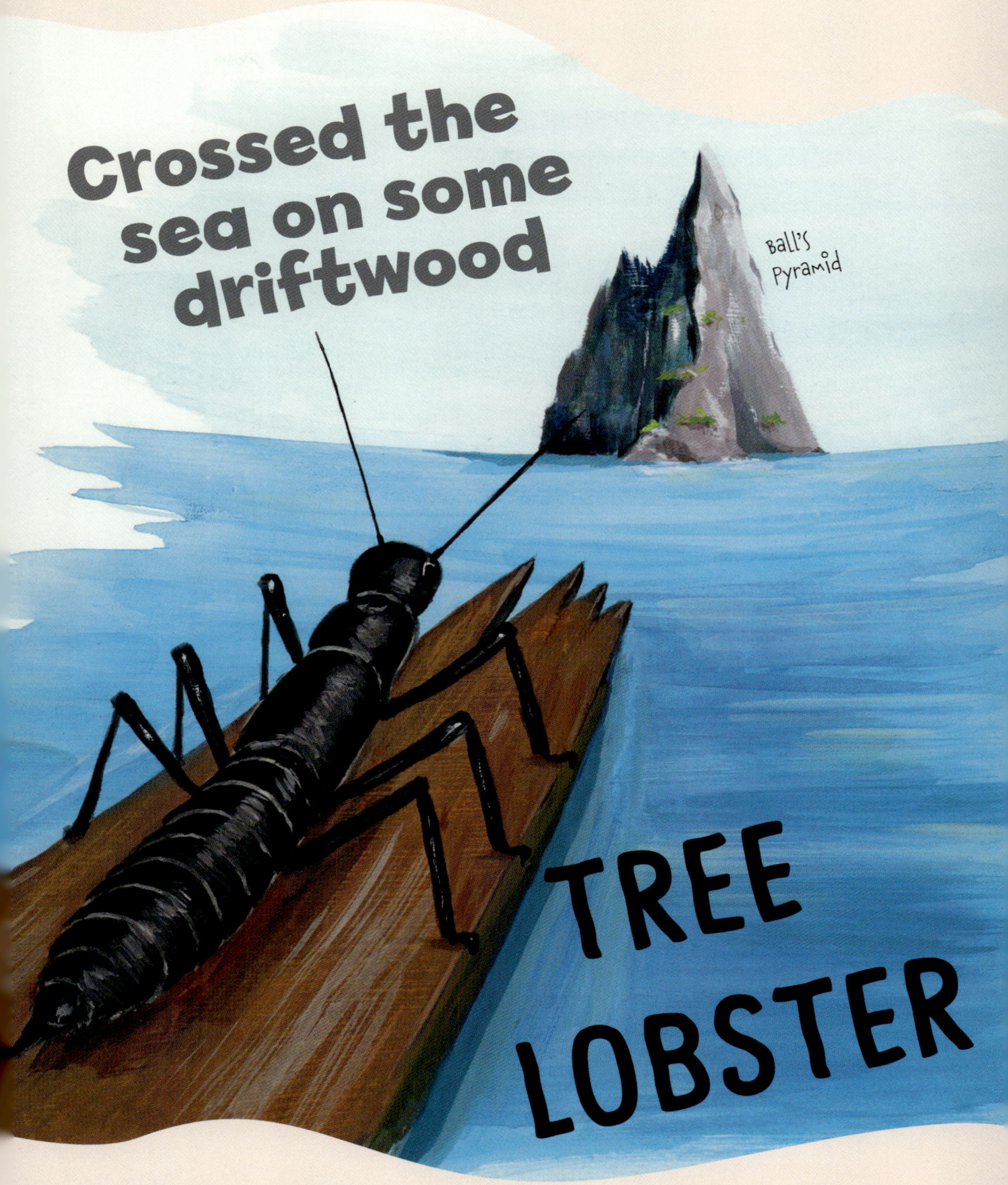
Crossed the sea on some driftwood
Ball's Pyramid
TREE LOBSTER

"The Lonely Coelacanth"
By Sheila Kanth

Once upon a time, there was a rather odd fish called coelacanth.

One day, coelacanth decided to dive thousands of feet deep down into the sea. His friends in the shallower water tried to stop him, but he took no notice.

"None of you can follow me!" he said proudly, and down he went.

Nobody did follow him. And he never came back to the shallow waters. He stayed in the deep, feeding on the fish and squid that lived there.

Time passed. Then, one day, he was caught in a fishing net, pulled up onto a boat, and taken to shore. Coelacanth was astonished by what he saw there. There were no dinosaurs. And animals called "humans" were swaggering about, as if they were in charge of everything.

It was only later that coelacanth heard that sixty-six million years before, a meteorite had hit the earth, killing all his old friends in the shallow waters.

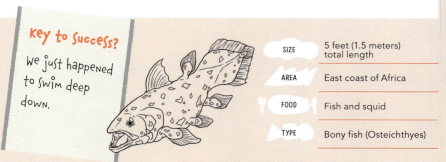

Key to success? We just happened to swim deep down.

SIZE	5 feet (1.5 meters) total length
AREA	East coast of Africa
FOOD	Fish and squid
TYPE	Bony fish (Osteichthyes)

Coelacanth-type fish flourished in the Carboniferous period in the Paleozoic era; it was thought that they had all died out at the end of the Cretaceous period (Mesozoic era). But then, in 1938, a living coelacanth was found. The coelacanths alive today are descendants of fish that happened to live deep in the sea, where the environment has been subject to little change. They were unaffected by the extinction events that impacted life on land and in shallow waters, and they remain almost the same as they were 350 million years ago.

(INCLUDES ALL COELACANTH-TYPE SPECIES)

PRECAMBRIAN | PALEOZOIC ERA (CAMBRIAN PERIOD, ORDOVICIAN PERIOD, SILURIAN PERIOD, DEVONIAN PERIOD, CARBONIFEROUS PERIOD, PERMIAN PERIOD) | MESOZOIC ERA (TRIASSIC PERIOD, JURASSIC PERIOD, CRETACEOUS PERIOD) | CENOZOIC ERA (PALEOGENE PERIOD, NEOGENE PERIOD, QUATERNARY PERIOD)

COELACANTH

Deeper and deeper

Strayed into the deep

Everyone on board, kids? Let's go home!

What is it? I'm busy! You want to know the trick of surviving? How should I know? I've got enough to think about, making sure this lot doesn't get hungry.

We'll eat anything to keep us alive. Fruit, insects, frogs, roadkill—whatever there is.

We're not fussy about where we live either. We started out in South America, but now some of us have reached as far as Canada.

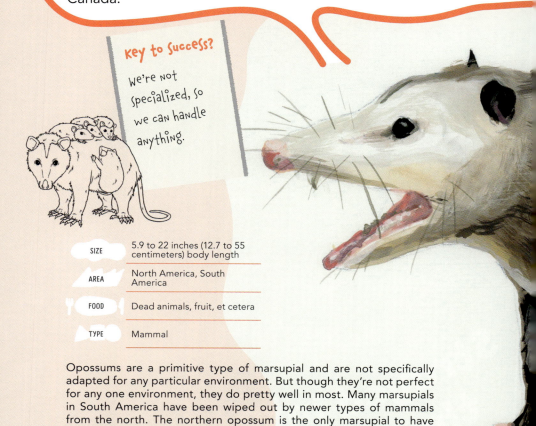

key to success?
We're not specialized, so we can handle anything.

SIZE	5.9 to 22 inches (12.7 to 55 centimeters) body length
AREA	North America, South America
FOOD	Dead animals, fruit, et cetera
TYPE	Mammal

Opossums are a primitive type of marsupial and are not specifically adapted for any particular environment. But though they're not perfect for any one environment, they do pretty well in most. Many marsupials in South America have been wiped out by newer types of mammals from the north. The northern opossum is the only marsupial to have gone the other direction, spreading into North America, where it can sometimes be seen in residential areas, rummaging through garbage.

We can walk on the ground, and we can climb trees. And we're not scared of water. Without that kind of can-do approach, we'd be goners.

The young of today! Always complaining! *Oh, the climate's changing*, they say. *Oh, I don't like the food*. They moan on and on. With attitudes like that they'll be beaten by the rats and go extinct! Don't blame "evolution" and "specialization." Just be like me—flexible—and do whatever you have to do to get things done!

Hang on tight!

Slow to evolve

OPOSSUM

Ha ha! You look like you don't believe me!

Well, I'm not surprised. After all, we lived in Lake Tazawa and were completely wiped out there seventy years ago. You humans were building a hydroelectric power plant and diverted a river into the lake. That changed the quality of the water, and fish like us died off.

But there'd been an experiment ten years earlier to find out if black kokanee eggs would develop in other lakes.

The experiment was thought to have failed. But actually, eggs that had been moved to another lake had developed into fish, and their descendants were discovered living there. How about that?

Ha ha ha! You can't touch us now! We're a classified endangered species.

You've got to protect us!

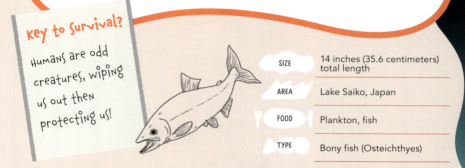

Key to survival?
Humans are odd creatures, wiping us out then protecting us!

SIZE	14 inches (35.6 centimeters) total length
AREA	Lake Saiko, Japan
FOOD	Plankton, fish
TYPE	Bony fish (Osteichthyes)

The black kokanee was endemic only to Lake Tazawa in Akita Prefecture, Japan. The construction of a hydroelectric plant led to changes in the water quality, and by 1948, the lake's black kokanee population had been wiped out. But it seems that in the 1930s fertilized black kokanee eggs had been transported to another site, and many years later it was discovered that the fish had survived in Lake Saiko in Yamanashi Prefecture. They were identified by a celebrity scientist called Mr. Fish, who wanted to draw a picture of a black kokanee. To help him do so, he ordered some live specimens of closely related kokanee salmon. But when they arrived, he found that some of the fish that had been supplied were in fact black kokanee!

BLACK KOKANEE

A lucky fish

Was somewhere else all along

Okay. Today I'm going to tell you how to make a burrow. There's not a lot of time, so let's get started.

First, *go down* into the soil. The water round here disappears in the dry season, so you've got to make your burrow before then. If you get your timing wrong, that could be fatal. Be careful!

Next, *curl up*. The point here is to have your head facing upward. That's the key to a beautiful burrow!

secret of survival?

keeping my skin moist with a mud pack.

1. Go down into soil
2. Curl up

How to burrow down
(INCLUDES ALL LUNGFISH-TYPE SPECIES)

SIZE	23 to 80 inches (58 to 203 centimeters) total length
AREA	Africa, South America, Australia
FOOD	Small fish, shrimps, shellfish
TYPE	Bony fish (Osteichthyes)

As its name suggests, a lungfish is a fish with lungs. It is a survivor of the sarcopterygii (fleshy finned fish) from which amphibians developed. Almost all other sarcopterygii became extinct, but the lungfish used their lungs to survive in rivers where ordinary fish could not—rivers that had very little water in the dry season. The African lungfish in particular has evolved to make burrows in the soil to prevent its skin drying out.

PRECAMBRIAN | PALEOZOIC ERA (CAMBRIAN PERIOD, ORDOVICIAN PERIOD, SILURIAN PERIOD, DEVONIAN PERIOD, CARBONIFEROUS PERIOD, PERMIAN PERIOD) | MESOZOIC ERA (TRIASSIC PERIOD, JURASSIC PERIOD, CRETACEOUS PERIOD) | CENOZOIC ERA (PALEOGENE PERIOD, NEOGENE PERIOD, QUATERNARY PERIOD)

And lastly, *harden the soil* with your mucus. You've got to produce that sticky stuff and spread it all around the soil in your burrow.

That's it! Once complete, your burrow is going to stop your body from getting too dry. All you have to do is just lie there and wait for the rainy season!

One last point: farmers sometimes dig up the soil. So watch out!

Stayed in a burrow

LUNGFISH

Afterword

This book has introduced a lot of reasons why animals have gone extinct. What did you think?

I expect a lot of readers are surprised at how many of the extinctions were caused by humans. But in those cases, we know for sure why the extinctions happened, because humans have kept records.

In most cases through Earth's history, we can't be certain why animals went extinct.

But by looking at fossil evidence, we know that particular animals existed in particular periods, and that the environment seems to have changed at particular times.

Researchers put together the evidence like pieces of a puzzle and imagine what the reasons for extinction were.

The reasons given for the extinctions of the animals in this book are not always certain, and especially for extinctions that happened a very long time ago, there are not many clues. In many cases, researchers have different opinions.

So for animals from the distant past whose extinction has not yet been fully explained, you can try and think up new theories yourselves!

I hope this book will encourage you to look at the world and its animals in a new way.

—TAKASHI MARUYAMA

INDEX

Creatures appearing in this book

A

Andrewsarchus—106

anomalocaris—76

archaeopteryx—70

argentavis—82

arsinoitherium—120

arthropleura—14

B

baiji (Chinese river dolphin)—100

black kokanee—144

bluebuck—46

Bonin grosbeak—10

bow-beaked Hawaiian honeycreeper—54

C

cameroceras—42

coelacanth—140

conodont—110

Cuban red macaw—114

D

diatryma—30

dickinsonia—22

dimetrodon—64
dodo—4
duck-billed platypus—128
dunkleosteus—80

G

giant moa—20
giant penguin—86
gigantopithecus—6
great auk—98
Guam flying fox—122

H

helicoprion—38

I

ichthyosaur—8
ichthyostega—92
Irish elk—52

J

Japanese wolf—26

L

laughing owl—116
lungfish—146
Lyall's wren—16

M

mamenchisaurus—66

mastodonsaurus—90

megalodon—74

meganeura—56

megatherium—32

N

nautilus—136

nipponites—44

O

opabinia—48

opossum—142

P

pakicetus—84

paraceratherium—78

passenger pigeon—40

pig-footed bandicoot—24

platybelodon—36

Polynesian tree snail—102

ptarmigan—130

pygmy hippopotamus—132

S

saber-toothed tiger (smilodon)—72

Schomburgk's deer—62

sea scorpion (eurypterid)—104

sivatherium—88

southern gastric-brooding frog—18

spinosaurus—12

stegosaurus—124

Steller's sea cow—2

T

tarpan—50

Tasmanian wolf—28

thylacosmilus—58

titanoboa—60

Toyotamaphimeia—108

tree lobster—138

trilobite—118

tuatara—134

tyrannosaurus—96

W

woolly mammoth—112

Quill Tree Books is an imprint of HarperCollins Publishers.

Why We Went Extinct
Text and art copyright © 2018 by Tadaaki Imaizumi and Takashi Maruyama
Translation copyright © 2024 by HarperCollins Publishers
Designer of original edition: Tae Nakamura
Cowriter: Ken Sawada
Coeditor: Eriko Tanaka
All rights reserved. Manufactured in Bosnia and Herzegovina.
No part of this book may be used or reproduced in any manner whatsoever without written permission except in the case of brief quotations embodied in critical articles and reviews. For information address HarperCollins Children's Books, a division of HarperCollins Publishers, 195 Broadway, New York, NY 10007.
www.harpercollinschildrens.com

Library of Congress Control Number: 2023948572
ISBN 978-0-06-308993-8

Typography by Torborg Davern and Kathy H. Lam
24 25 26 27 28 GPS 10 9 8 7 6 5 4 3 2 1

Originally published in 2018 in Japanese by Diamond Inc.